Cambridge Elements ≡

Elements in Crime Narratives
edited by
Margot Douaihy
Emerson College
Catherine Nickerson
Emory College of Arts and Sciences
Henry Sutton
University of East Anglia

FORENSIC CRIME FICTION

Aliki Varvogli
University of Dundee

CAMBRIDGE
UNIVERSITY PRESS

Shaftesbury Road, Cambridge CB2 8EA, United Kingdom

One Liberty Plaza, 20th Floor, New York, NY 10006, USA

477 Williamstown Road, Port Melbourne, VIC 3207, Australia

314–321, 3rd Floor, Plot 3, Splendor Forum, Jasola District Centre,
New Delhi – 110025, India

103 Penang Road, #05–06/07, Visioncrest Commercial, Singapore 238467

Cambridge University Press is part of Cambridge University Press & Assessment,
a department of the University of Cambridge.

We share the University's mission to contribute to society through the pursuit of
education, learning and research at the highest international levels of excellence.

www.cambridge.org
Information on this title: www.cambridge.org/9781009517249

DOI: 10.1017/9781009365918

First published 2024

A catalogue record for this publication is available from the British Library.

ISBN 978-1-009-51724-9 Hardback
ISBN 978-1-009-36590-1 Paperback
ISSN 2755-1873 (online)
ISSN 2755-1865 (print)

Forensic Crime Fiction

Elements in Crime Narratives

DOI: 10.1017/9781009365918
First published online: June 2024

Aliki Varvogli
University of Dundee

Author for correspondence: Aliki Varvogli, a.varvogli@dundee.ac.uk

Abstract: This study of forensic crime fiction from the US and the UK examines the prominent roles that women play in many of these novels, arguing that there are historical continuities with earlier forms of contact with the dead body. Refuting claims that the female forensic examiner exhibits traits of typically masculine behaviour, it suggests that the female gaze humanises the victims of crime and alters their representations. Utilising the views of a world-famous forensic scientist interviewed for this Element, this study also explores the role and treatment of science in forensic crime fiction, shedding light on this area of the genre. Finally, there is consideration of killers in forensic crime novels, proposing that the relationship between killer and investigator is different from that of the classic crime novel. There are also two appendices containing interviews with Professor Niamh Nic Daeid and with Val McDermid.

Keywords: forensic crime fiction, crime novel, detective fiction, science and literature, Patricia Cornwell

ISBNs: 9781009517249 (HB), 9781009365901 (PB), 9781009365918 (OC)
ISSNs: 2755-1873 (online), 2755-1865 (print)

Contents

Introduction

A grisly crime has taken place: two women, mother and daughter, have been brutally murdered in their own home. The crime scene suggests the use of force and carries strong hints of sexually motivated violence. There is broken furniture, a razor smeared with blood, and long strands of human hair. One of the bodies is found to have scratches, bruises, and deep indentations of fingernails, while the other has had her throat cut. With so much forensic evidence left on the scene, how hard will it be to catch the killer? Given that the crime scene is, of course, the apartment in the Rue Morgue, we know that Auguste Dupin solves the crime that all of Parisian society considers 'an insoluble mystery'.[1] Dupin has access to the same evidence as the police, and yet he is able to construct a different hypothesis from them and test it to arrive at the truth. It is therefore not the material evidence itself that points to the killer, but rather the imagination and intuition of this enigmatic figure who is able to 'see' the story of the crime that was invisible to everyone else. With 'The Murders in the Rue Morgue' (1841), Poe is credited with the creation of the analytical detective story, but he created much more than that. Poe invented the concept of the lone genius detective who solves crime not because he is immersed in a world of criminality, but because he is removed from it. He also invented the clue, taking an idea that had currency in intellectual circles amongst the Transcendentalists and applying it to the crime story. Most crucially, his choice of female victims expressed both his own conviction that the death of a beautiful woman is the most poetic subject in the world (and, therefore, the death of older or unattractive women is fair game in the crime story, where no one seems to care very much for their demise) and established a blueprint that is still followed today.[2] Crime fiction has evolved significantly, shifting the focus on the female victims in ways that have progressed from the fetishisation of the dead female to a consideration of gender-based violence and the social causes of crime. Nevertheless, the dead, mutilated, or violated female as the starting point of an investigation remains a powerful trope, and the fascination with the traumatised female body persists, still to be found at the centre of a significant proportion of fictional forensic investigations.

The central premises of the female victim, the disordered crime scene, and the sexual violence element are so familiar as tropes in forensic crime fiction that it

---

[1] E. A. Poe, 'The Murders in the Rue Morgue', in *The Complete Tales and Poems of Edgar Allan Poe* (London: Penguin, 1982), p. 152.

[2] In 'The philosophy of composition', Poe writes: 'the death, then, of a beautiful woman is, unquestionably, the most poetical topic in the world'. The Project Gutenberg eBook of 'The raven' and 'The philosophy of composition', by Edgar Allan Poe (www.gutenberg.org/cache/epub/55749/pg55749-images.html).

is easy to overlook how fresh and unusual they were when Edgar Allan Poe wrote 'The Murders in the Rue Morgue' and, in so doing, gave birth not only to crime fiction as a genre, but also to forensic crime fiction as a sub-genre. Many critics point out that Poe gave birth to a 'flawed' version of the crime story: the first criminal is a force of nature, and the crime has no motive, for example. Therefore, neither the solution to the mystery nor the resolution of the plot offer the traditional restoration of order that we have come to expect of the crime story. In a similar vein, it can also be argued that Poe invented the rebuttal of the forensic crime story, ironically embedded within a forensic crime story. This can be seen more clearly in 'The Purloined Letter', where Monsieur G, the Prefect of the Parisian police, gives an account of the exhaustive search they have conducted in order to recover a compromising letter from Minister D's house. An increasingly incredulous Dupin asks the Prefect whether they have taken apart all the furniture, all the soft furnishings, opened every package and parcel, looked under the floorboards. The Prefect assures him that they have done all that and much more: 'We divided its [the apartment's] entire surface into compartments, which we numbered, so that none might be missed; then we scrutinized each individual square inch throughout the premises.' They also employed a 'most powerful microscope': 'Had there been any traces of recent disturbance we should not have failed to detect it instantly. A single grain of gimlet-dust, for example, would have been as obvious as an apple.'[3] Their method of investigation is impressive for both its thoroughness and the sophistication of the equipment used, but still it yields no results. Therefore, both stories suggest that forensic evidence alone cannot solve a crime, and that the powers of empathy and imagination are superior to the scrutiny of empirical, material evidence.

Dupin solves the mystery of the purloined letter because he knows and can therefore recreate his opponent's intellectual and emotional state; as the narrator observes, '[i]t is merely . . . an identification of the reasoner's intellect with that of his opponent.'[4] Poe, therefore, not only invented crime story clues, he also demonstrated their limitations in crime investigation. He believed that science was placing too much emphasis on material evidence, ignoring other ways of understanding human behaviour, such as empathy or moral imagination. In his 'Sonnet – to Science', he berates science's 'peering eyes' that prey upon the poet's heart, altering things to 'dull realities'.[5] In the poem, as in his fiction, dull realities are the realities of the material world that are available to us through empirical evidence. They are dull because they do not account for the powers of

---

[3] Poe, 'The Purloined Letter', in *The Complete Tales*, pp. 211–13.   [4] Ibid., p. 215.
[5] Poe, 'Sonnet – to Science' in *The Complete Tales*, p. 992.

the imagination that Poe and his contemporaries championed. Yet it is these dull realities that are proving to be a source of ongoing fascination in crime fiction today. Advances in forensic science, and also in special effects for film and TV, have made science much more appealing, accessible, and fascinating for writers and their audiences. In addition to the continued popularity of forensic crime fiction, non-fiction is also becoming a popular genre; Val McDermid's *Forensics: The Anatomy of Crime* (2014) is an unusual but popular example of a novelist who took to non-fiction to communicate some of the thrills of forensic science, while forensic scientists such as Sue Black and Richard Shepherd borrow elements from fiction in order to create vivid and engaging accounts of the application of forensic science. When asked, in an interview conducted for this Element, about 'the forensic turn' in crime fiction, Val McDermid replied that all crime fiction is now forensic fiction, because it has become routine to use forensic evidence to solve crime, and because it has also become harder to solve crime without it.[6] The generic transition was gradual for a long time, but it accelerated in the 1990s with the appearance of Patricia Cornwell's Kay Scarpetta novels. Since then, forensic crime fiction has continued to grow in popularity, and the shifts in investigative methods from older types of crime fiction have created the need to redefine the genre in terms of its gender politics, its attitudes to science and reason, and its depictions of criminality. These three areas form the basis of the current study.

The traditional narrative of the evolution of crime fiction suggests that, after Poe, the genre moved in two directions: in the US, hardboiled fiction gained dominance, whereas British literature perfected the analytical crime puzzle. Hardboiled fiction had little use for forensic evidence; its emphasis on unfolding action, uncertainty, and precarity was at odds with the practice of collecting and analysing clues. Therefore, clues played a marginal role in stories by Hammett, Chandler, and their descendants, with action dominating the plot instead. In the analytical crime story most closely associated with the British tradition, clues were given prominence, with Agatha Christie and Dorothy L. Sayers both using their knowledge of chemistry and pharmaceuticals to construct elaborate plots and include dramatic scenes of death by poison. These two approaches to crime writing offer contrasting views on fundamental questions, such as the availability of objective, empirically derived truth, the conviction that we live in world that makes sense, or the belief that stories can offer comfort and reassurance. What the two sub-genres had in common, though, was a distrust of the police

---

[6] I take the term 'forensic turn' from Lindsay Steenberg, who proposes it in *Forensic Science in Contemporary American Popular Culture: Gender, Crime, and Science* (London: Routledge, 2013). The full interview with Val McDermid can be found in Appendix 2; further references to the interview are also taken from Appendix 2.

force and an emphasis on the charismatic individual who, like Poe's Dupin, was better at solving crime and often exposed the inadequacies of organised law enforcement. Following the golden age of both hardboiled fiction and the analytical crime story, the police procedural absorbed elements from both and became the dominant genre. As the investigation of crime became ever more sophisticated and specialised, amateurs and free-lance investigators no longer had access to the resources that are needed to solve crime. Forensic crime fiction relies on official structures and organisations and therefore needs to involve the police force. At the same time, though, much forensic crime fiction retains the mistrust or disdain for the police found in earlier iterations of the genre. Therefore, there will often be a scientist who takes centre stage, conducting an investigation that is sometimes aided but often also hampered by the police. This, in turn, means that the forensic crime novel is not necessarily a type of police procedural, though the two share many traits involving the systematic analysis of material evidence through organised structures and official channels. Kerstin Bergman notes that in 'police procedurals and hard-boiled detective novels, the truth is sometimes avoided, neglected, and/or concealed, because this is considered best for society as a whole', whereas the 'scientist in the forensic subgenre ... has an obligation to stick to the truth'.[7] Whilst the police procedural is often used as a vehicle for critique of law enforcement, forensic crime fiction does not call into question the integrity of the scientists. It does often portray attempts, by criminals but also by the police, to discredit the scientist, thereby further legitimising the function of the latter in the genre and, by implication, in society as well. The figure of the scientist who is sometimes in peril because of their commitment to the truth stands in stark contrast to the corrupt police officer who is a familiar trope in hardboiled fiction and in the police procedural.

Despite the difficulties inherent in all attempts to categorise a group of novels in terms of genre or sub-genre, it is easy to see why the study of forensic crime fiction is aided by the assumption that such a category of fiction does exist. As this study will go on to demonstrate, earlier works of forensic fiction from the 1990s can be read as examples of what Deborah Jermyn usefully calls the process of 'generic renewal'.[8] Since then, forensic science has progressed to an extent that even the early adopters could not have foreseen and, as a result, it is now harder to speak of forensic crime fiction because there's very little crime fiction that does *not* use scientific evidence. Even though nearly all crime fiction

---

[7] K. Bergman, 'Fictional death and scientific truth: The truth-value of science in contemporary forensic crime fiction', *Clues: A Journal of Detection*, 30.1 (Spring 2012), 88–98 (90).
[8] D. Jermyn, 'Labs and slabs: Television crime drama and the quest for forensic realism', *Studies in History and Philosophy of Biological and Biomedical Sciences*, 44 (2013), 103–9 (103).

has a degree of familiarity with forensic investigations, it is still useful to draw some faint lines, rather than hard boundaries, that will allow us to focus on particular types of crime fiction. For the purposes of the present study, which focuses on British and North American fiction, I used the following as my guide: a novel should be classified as forensic crime fiction if most of these conditions are met: the use of forensic investigation is presented in considerable, extensive, sustained, and scientifically plausible detail; a forensic scientist is a major character in the book; and forensic evidence plays a key role in the resolution of the plot and the unveiling and apprehension of the culprits.

The origins of genres and sub-genres are always contested, but Patricia Cornwell's *Postmortem* (1990) is a good candidate for the claim that it originated forensic crime fiction. The novel not only created a blueprint that Cornwell herself used in her subsequent Scarpetta novels, it also laid down some generic parameters that other writers continue to follow. The novel introduced Kay Scarpetta, medical examiner and narrator of her story. The first few pages alone contain several tropes that are now widely recognised as hallmarks of the forensic crime novel. The narrative opens with Scarpetta dreaming of 'a face formless and inhuman like the faces of misshapen dolls', 'an evil intelligence' outside her window looking in.[9] This is significant in many ways. It introduces the preoccupation with evil that runs throughout the series, casting Scarpetta in the role of the saviour who expunges evil through the application of rational scientific enquiry. Further, the notion that the evil presence is on the outside looking in places the medical examiner at the heart of the story: she is at the centre of it and is the recipient of the evil gaze, rather than being the one who looks out of the metaphorical window in order to comprehend and apprehend evil. In addition, throughout the series Scarpetta is depicted as a character who feels constantly under threat, and who is hyper-aware of security around her fortress-like house. The idea that women are under threat by home intruders is one that the forensic novel often promotes; it is a way of sensationalising gender-based violence and obscuring the more disturbing truth that women are most threatened by the men they live with, rather than strangers lurking in the shadows around the home. Much of the appeal of this and other types of crime fiction comes precisely from this discrepancy between the lived experience of violence and the type of violence depicted in these novels. Later in the opening sequence, Scarpetta is awoken from her dream by the sound of the phone ringing, an event that causes her heart to feel like it is 'drilling through [her] ribs'.[10] The admission of vulnerability and fear is another hallmark of the sub-genre. Whereas both police officers and private eyes are depicted as tough

---

[9] P. Cornwell, *Postmortem* (London: Warner, 1990), p. 3. [10] Ibid.

characters (and this would include women such as Kinsey Millhone and V. I. Warshawski), the forensic scientist has neither the training nor the attitude that accompanies the image of the tough or fearless crime-fighting investigator. In the opening pages of *Postmortem*, it is also notable that the victim is introduced as an attractive and successful white woman in her thirties. Women are disproportionately represented in the forensic novel, both as victims and as forensic scientists, and some of the implications of this phenomenon will be examined in Section 1. Scarpetta also hints at a troubled relationship with Sergeant Marino, a character who made his debut as a homophobic, possibly misogynistic law enforcer, but who grows and changes as the series unfolds. The pairing of a forensic scientist with a homicide detective is another powerful trope, often used by writers with a strong emphasis on gendered behaviours and conflicts.

Assuming we have identified some generic parameters for forensic crime fiction, what questions might we ask of the (sub-)genre? Some will overlap with questions that we ask of any type of crime novel, while others will be more specific to the sub-genre. For example, one question that has preoccupied critics is the crime genre's status vis-à-vis the status quo: does crime fiction on the whole reinforce state controls and dominant ideologies, or does it seek to undermine them? Ronald R. Thomas and Andrew Pepper are two critics who have deepened our understanding of the crime novel's complex and often conflicting attitudes to criminality and law enforcement. Thomas notes that '[d]etective fiction as a form is generally recognized as an invention of the nineteenth century, coincident with the development of the modern police force and the creation of the modern bureaucratic state.' He goes on to argue that the crime novel does not merely reflect the reality of modern police forces, but also that it performs 'cultural work . . . for societies that were increasingly preoccupied with systematically bringing under control the potentially anarchic forces unleashed by democratic reform'.[11] His subsequent analysis of nineteenth-century crime fiction focuses on the tensions between 'particular political anxieties' and the types of inquiry and knowledge that such anxieties necessitated.[12] Pepper concurs that the crime genre is deeply implicated with 'the consolidation of the modern, bureaucratic state . . . with the policing, governmental, and judicial apparatuses set up to enforce the law'.[13] His nuanced argument reads crime fiction as both sustaining the status quo and

---

[11] R. R. Thomas, *Detective Fiction and the Rise of Forensic Science* (Cambridge University Press, 1999), p. 4.

[12] Ibid., p. 6.

[13] A. Pepper, *Unwilling Executioner: Crime Fiction and the State* (Oxford University Press, 2016), p. 1.

also undermining its own conservative impulse 'by the crime story's typical refusal to turn a blind eye to institutional failure and corruption'.[14] Forensic crime fiction is a fine testing ground for Pepper's hypothesis. Material evidence, as Thomas shows, showcases the narrative of objectivity and, by implication, the infallibility of law enforcement. On the other hand, the element of human interpretation inherent in forensic science has the potential to undermine the fantasy of an objective, external reality measurable in microscopic evidence. The forensic crime novel thrives on this tension and continues to raise questions about epistemology and about our need for conclusive forensic evidence and for satisfying narrative resolution.

A question that is specific to the forensic crime novel is that of graphic depictions of extreme violence. These are not unique to the genre, of course, but what makes the study of them particularly interesting is that they are often to be found alongside descriptions of autopsies or other depictions of the examination of human remains that are equally graphic. The forensic novel relies on creating a balance between the two: using the human body as a site of abjection, but also as a site of redemption. The depictions of extreme violence dehumanise the victims of crime and show that this dehumanisation is often one of the killer's primary motives. The forensic examination of a dead, tortured, and mutilated body is also dehumanising in a different way: it takes the body of the deceased and turns it into a series of organs to be examined and sections of the body to be scrutinised. The mutilated body is thus further torn apart in the course of the investigation. The crucial difference is that the forensic taking apart of the body has the ultimate aim of putting it back together again. When an autopsy is concluded, the body is literally put together again as organs are returned and incisions are closed. It is also put together metaphorically because the pathologist, working with the police, uses the body to read and reconstruct the story of the crime and to restore peace and order to the disordered world of criminality. The forensic novel's preoccupation with graphic violence and descriptions of mutilated and dissected bodies also needs to be understood within a gendered framework. Section 1 examines the role of female pathologists and other scientists, as well as the role of the female victims that dominate the genre. Sections 2 and 3 examine the role of science in the restoration of order, and the attitudes to criminality that can be gleaned from depictions of the imaginative sadistic killers who are also a strong feature of the genre. The focus is on novels that have been selected as exemplary in two senses of the word: they are amongst the best of their type, but also the conclusions concerning these novels can equally be applied or tested against other examples of the genre.

---

[14] Ibid., p. 2.

1 Raising the Dead: A Woman's Work?

When Patricia Cornwell's chief medical examiner Dr Kay Scarpetta made her debut in 1990, few could have predicted that the female professional would come to dominate the sub-genre of forensic crime fiction. Real-life accounts of forensic pathologists were exclusively male, and, as Scarpetta often claimed in the novels, being any kind of medical expert meant being in a minority and working in a male-dominated environment. Therefore, *Postmortem* and subsequent novels in the series made a dual contribution: Scarpetta broke new ground by having a leading role as a female chief medical examiner in a male-dominated world, and the solving of murder through the examination of the body and other material evidence overtook other forms of detection to become the dominant mode of inquiry. The female investigator and the dazzling use of newly discovered methods for analysing material evidence are now major features of forensic crime fiction, and the relationship between the two is still the focus of critical enquiry.

Cornwell was following a well-trodden path in her depictions of sadistic killers, extreme violence, and the mystery of what motivates some criminals to operate so far outside the bounds of societal norms. Yet, where much of the depiction of violence had previously focused on unfolding action, here it became a post-mortem depiction. The hardboiled novel, for example, relies on violent confrontation between criminals, and between criminals and the police. Graphic depictions of violence often become a means of driving the plot, and are used to heighten suspense. With its emphasis on unfolding action, though, the hardboiled novel has little opportunity to focus on the victims of crime. Dashiell Hammett's *Red Harvest*, which set a blueprint for the genre, famously has a chapter called 'The Seventeenth Murder', which serves as a reminder that the thrill of the body count is more important to the hardboiled novel than the reality of violence inflicted on the body. Similarly, the police procedural places emphasis on the investigation as a mystery that needs to be solved. The victims of crime originate the plot and the investigation, but they are not necessarily of interest as people who have lost their lives. In some ways, then, hardboiled fiction and police procedurals predating Cornwell still perpetuate the formula introduced by Edgar Allan Poe. The female victims in 'The Murders in the Rue Morgue' were little more than plot devices that allowed Dupin's superior powers of observation and analysis to shine, and the identity of the culprit, who turns out to be an orangutang, received a much lengthier account than the identities of the victims.[15]

---

[15] Notable exceptions can be found outside the anglophone tradition. For example, *Roseanna* (1965), by Maj Sjöwall and Per Wahlöö, builds a picture of murder victim Roseanna McGraw

Dr Scarpetta also possesses superior powers of observation and analysis, but she brought something new to crime fiction: care and compassion for the victims of crime, and identification with the victim, which stands in stark opposition to Dupin's identification with the intellect of his opponent in 'The Purloined Letter'. The fact that she is a medical expert rather than a law enforcer is crucial here. Before forensic crime fiction, investigators were of two types. Some were individuals outside the organised police force, such as gifted amateurs or private eyes, who had varying degrees of commitment to the restoration of law and order. Amateur sleuths would solve crimes as a form of entertainment, almost – a means of intellectual gratification. Private investigators (PIs) would often generate at least as much criminal activity as they were trying to stamp out, and their relationship to police departments was always fraught at best, antagonistic at worst. Investigators within police departments, on the other hand, were bound by the strictures of law and tasked with delivering results with the main purpose of bringing criminals to justice, even if they had to bend the rules to achieve results. Traditionally, the crime novel ends with the identification and apprehension of the culprit. Classic crime fiction, paradoxically, has little time for what comes afterwards: the trial, the punishment, or the sense of relief and retribution for the families of the victims. By making her main investigator an agent of medicine and science rather than the law, Cornwell shifted the emphasis and opened up new possibilities for imagining the relationship between investigator and crime victim.

Jun-nan Chou argues that the body

> is important in women's crime fiction because it provides a perspective nearer to that of the victim and his/her body, in contrast to the kind of police procedural novel that is focused on the psyche of the killer. Women's crime fiction has two other features that distinguish it from its police procedural counterpart: the female forensic pathologist's 'affective' view of the dead and her becoming an intended victim herself.[16]

In real life, police officers are much more likely to be threatened, wounded, or killed in the line of duty than medical examiners. Also, in the real world, the work of the medical examiner and other forensic scientists remains invisible until the case is brought to court; after all, that is the meaning of the adjective 'forensic' in the first place. Reality doesn't always make good fiction, though, and in taking liberties that cast the pathologist in the role of the investigator

---

gradually, so that the emergence of her character is shown to be one of the outcomes of the police investigation.

[16] J. Chou, 'Seeing bones speaking: The female gaze and the posthuman embodiment in Reichs's forensic crime fiction', *Concentric: Literary and Cultural Studies*, 38.1 (March 2012) 145–69 (145).

crime novelists not only furnish us with plots and characters that are more interesting than their real-life counterparts might have been, they also create truths that have cultural resonance even when they are not supported by hard evidence.

The focus of Dr Scarpetta's first case in *Postmortem* is a recently graduated physician. 'She. Lori Petersen. Brown. Harvard. Brilliant. Thirty years old. About to have it all realized, her dream. After eight grueling years, at least, of medical training. A physician. All of it destroyed in a few minutes.'[17] The syncopated sentences and unusual syntax betray Scarpetta's strong emotional reaction to the case, which stems from an identification with the victim. At the crime scene, she notices that the living room 'was immaculate, and attractively decorated in warm rose tones';[18] in stark contrast to the disorder of the apartment in the Rue Morgue, this is a tasteful home such as the one that Scarpetta herself occupies. Scarpetta's domestic space is used throughout the series, serving a variety of purposes. It allows Cornwell to show that there is conflict between Scarpetta's private and public selves, stemming from her presence as a woman in a male-dominated environment. It also gives the author an opportunity to inject some extra femininity into her character by depicting some rare moments of domestic contentment. At the same time, though, the home becomes a place of danger in many of the novels, and those early experiences of Scarpetta dealing with victims who were attacked by home intruders provide an explanation for her own insecurity and fear in her otherwise much-prized domestic space. Announcing from the outset her desire to distance herself from the type of crime novel that reduces the female victim to the function of a corpse, Cornwell has Scarpetta remark that 'these murdered women were the colleagues you sit next to at work, the friends you invite to go shopping or to stop by for drinks'.[19] This statement is also interesting for the types of women it excludes, but it does nevertheless suggest that the medical examiner cares for them in a way that her police partner, Sergeant Marino, almost certainly doesn't.

As first-person narrator, Scarpetta is also given ample opportunity to reflect on attitudes to the victims of violence. Her descriptions of the crime scene in the opening pages, which are more conventionally aimed at the reader, are interspersed with more private reflections on female victimhood: 'there would be thoughts, remarks about her physical attributes or lack of them. There would be sophomoric jokes and cynical asides as the victim, not the killer, went on trial, every aspect of her person and the way she lived, scrutinized, judged and, in some instances, degraded.'[20] The identification is therefore not only with women who were just like her before they were killed, but also with the fact

---

[17] Cornwell, *Postmortem*, p. 8.   [18] Ibid.   [19] Ibid.   [20] Ibid., p. 10.

that, as female victims of violence, they will be apportioned blame. The medical examiner's concern for the female victims – by which I mean both their suffering and the conditions of their victimhood – intensifies in the second novel in the series, *Body of Evidence*, where Scarpetta becomes almost obsessed with the question of why her victim opened the door to let her killer in. Scarpetta is depicted as living in a high-security home, and is often anxious about being attacked herself. Therefore, having to confront the reality of another woman who fell victim to the threat that haunts her brings a strong sense of identification with the victim, and a desire to restore justice not only in order to prevent further crime but also to regain a sense of security and control in her own domestic space. Alongside her desire to solve the mystery, Scarpetta also needs to restore a narrative that suggests the victim was not the author of her own misfortune, that she did not invite the violence upon herself by opening the door. The novel's climactic scene reinforces the analogy, as Scarpetta herself opens the door to an assailant; a fierce battle ensues and, in killing him, she defends her home, avenges the death of her victim, and proves that the victims (herself included) were not to blame.

The emphasis on domesticity, fear, and female solidarity needs to be further considered along with other gendered depictions and critical readings of Scarpetta as a pioneering character in the genre. Using the work of Ludmilla Jordanova and Kathleen Gregory Klein, Joy Palmer argues that, before Cornwell more or less invented the forensic crime novel as we know it today, the crime novel was a 'masculinist' genre because it relied on an empiricist investigative gaze that was culturally gendered male.[21] Palmer argues that 'Cornwell's decision to portray her protagonist within such masculinist conventions clearly raises significant questions about the ideological or feminist impetus of her work', but concludes that Cornwell's conservative attitudes to matters such as sexuality and the social causes of crime disqualify her from the role of feminist subverter of the genre. 'Though the author depicts Dr Scarpetta as a single, strong-minded, and zealously independent woman', writes Palmer, 'the series' overall ambivalent attitude towards gender and sexuality, and its ultimately conservative position on criminality and social deviancy, renders Cornwell an unlikely candidate for "sister in crime"'.[22] However, a different reading of the Scarpetta novels may be arrived at if we consider Cornwell not as an author who inserts a female character into a masculinist tradition, but rather as someone who creates an entirely new sub-genre precisely in order to query and subvert the idea that crime is solved through the persistence of the male or

---

[21] J. Palmer, 'Tracing bodies: Gender, genre, and forensic detective fiction', *South Central Review*, 18.3/4 (Autumn–Winter 2001), 54–71 (56).

[22] Ibid., 57.

masculinist penetrative gaze. Sara Paretsky's V. I. Warshawski and Sue Grafton's Kinsey Millhone are both given gender-neutral names in an attempt to draw attention to the difficulties of being female PIs in a male-dominated world and a predominantly masculinist genre. Both authors give them attributes and actions that set them apart from their male counterparts, but because they are PIs they still need to operate within the parameters of the genre. Therefore, it could be argued that Paretsky and Grafton altered the genre, but they did not reimagine it. Cornwell went a step further by creating a new role, one that allowed her to have a female protagonist who was not taking on a function previously assigned to men within the conventions of the genre.

Another generic renovation can be found in Cornwell's interest in dead female bodies. Before Cornwell, the female body was the originator of the plot, but not the focus of the investigation. By placing the mutilated female body at the heart of Scarpetta's cases, Cornwell proposed a different investigative method that did not rely on the penetrative gaze, but rather emphasised the need for a skillset that was different to that of the detective. Glen S. Close has written persuasively of 'the gendering and sexualization of the cadaver' in a generic tendency that he identifies as 'necropornography'. Close finds in crime fiction 'a fascination not only with beautiful female corpses but also with autopsies and morgues'.[23] Close's extensive treatment of the subject of necropornography starts with Poe and moves on to the hardboiled tradition and its displays of misogyny, but forensic fiction of the 1990s and beyond is not within the scope of his enquiry. He concludes with the assertion that 'female cadavers are eroticized by reference to the past sexual behavior of the dead women and in scenes in which male forensic and medical authorities inspect naked female corpses'.[24] Does the creation of female forensic and medial authorities alter these generic conventions? As with any modification to the genre that steers it away from its original focus on white masculinities, the question that critics have asked is whether Scarpetta and her peers behave in ways that align them with their male predecessors, or whether their presence significantly alters the fundamental, underlying attitudes and ideologies of the crime novel. Scarpetta contains elements that can support both approaches. She feels vulnerable to male intruders at home and undermined by powerful males in her professional life, but at the same time she possesses skills and powers that far exceed those of her male detective companion. Sabine Vanacker argues that Scarpetta

---

[23] G. S. Close, *Female Corpses in Crime fiction: A Transatlantic Perspective* (London: Palgrave, 2018), p. 35.

[24] Ibid. p. 86

functions in the reader's emotional field like a Dr Frankenstein in reverse, unpicking what used to be a living body into its component parts. Not only does she assume the unselfquestioning activity of the male detective's unified subject position – her actions are indeed determined, confident and incisive – but she also departs considerably from the traditional constraints and qualities associated with her gender. Rather than being culturally associated (as female) with life and life giving, this woman hero is a dealer in death, who aggressively 'manhandles' the corpses of victims and gruesomely thrives off decaying and decomposing bodies.[25]

Vanacker concludes that 'Cornwell uses Scarpetta to subvert traditional gender roles which associate femininity … with the giving of life.'[26] Whereas Vanacker is right to note that Scarpetta's work demands the physical and emotional strength more commonly associated with the male hero, her reading of Scarpetta glosses over the medical examiner's empathy for her victims, and overlooks Scarpetta's desire to shield them from further harm on the autopsy table. More crucially, Vanacker's reading relies on the image of the pathologist as a dealer in death, whereas Scarpetta can be more fruitfully seen as the figurative restorer of life.

The identification of human remains or the examination of murder victims' bodies are harrowing tasks that force us to confront mortality, the fragile materiality of our existence, and the human capacity for violence. The pathologist imposes order on the seemingly random acts of violence and murder by examining the body and using evidence to read the crime. By rendering the objectified body legible, the pathologist both contains the violence and begins to restore the humanity of the victim. The murder victim is given a voice by the pathologist, and the violated, mutilated body transforms from a site of violence and brutalisation to one that leads to healing and recovery (of the crime story, and of the victim's humanity). Figuratively speaking, the pathologist reanimates the body by allowing it to tell its story. This helps to counteract the abjection inherent in treating the body as flesh, or material evidence. These symbolic transformations recall the story of Frankenstein that Vanacker alludes to, and help us to understand the centrality of women in this line of work: the pathologist 'gives life' to the victim while also tending to the body in an intimate way that is more closely associated with care-giving than with death. Historically the two functions – the care for the body and the dissection of the body – can be divided along gendered lines. Katherine Howell notes that the 'central procedures of autopsy and dissection have historically been seen as abominations',

[25] S. Vanacker, 'V. I. Warshawski, Kinsey Millhone and Kay Scarpetta: Creating a Feminist Detective Hero' in P. B. Messent (ed.), *Criminal Proceedings: The Contemporary American Crime Novel* (Chicago, IL: Pluto Press, 1997), pp. 62–77 (p. 66)

[26] Ibid. p. 67

because they contradicted the idea of the human body as constructed in Abrahamic theology.[27] Remnants of the belief that autopsy and dissection are assaults on the humanity of the person as ordained by God can be found in modern attitudes to the body as having the potential to be further 'violated' by exhumation, autopsy, or other post-mortem investigations. The washing and caring of the dead, on the other hand, have been seen as obligations performed by women and symbolically aimed at asserting the humanity of the bodily remains.

One of the most striking ways in which we can understand both the evolution of religious beliefs surrounding the dead body over time and the significance of the gendered gaze is by looking at Rembrandt's 'Anatomy Lesson of Dr Nicolaes Tulp' of 1632. The famous painting, housed in the Mauritshuis Museum in the Hague, Netherlands, invites the viewer's gaze to focus on the pallid corpse at the lower centre of the canvas, its whiteness providing a stark contrast to, and seemingly also illuminating, the black-clad doctors who surround it. Unlike the gaze of the spectator, which is drawn to the corpse, Dr Tulp's gaze is, improbably, not directed at the body as he conducts his anatomy lesson. The anatomist's averted gaze represents his mastery over the subject: he knows the muscles and tendons so well that he hardly needs to look at them to do his job well. At the same time, the averted gaze hints at the disassociation between the anatomist and the body: Dr Tulp is conducting a lesson for the benefit of the men surrounding the corpse and they are the deserving recipients of his gaze, rather than the corpse used for demonstration. Finally, the averted gaze hints at the terror of abjection. The painting both invites us to look at the flesh beneath the skin and depicts the averted gaze that symbolically recoils from the abject. 'The corpse', Julia Kristeva writes, 'is cesspool, and death; it upsets even more violently the one who confronts it . . . [R]efuse and corpses *show me* what I permanently thrust aside in order to live. These body fluids, this defilement, this shit are what life withstands, hardly and with difficulty, on the part of death.'[28] Dr Tulp therefore looks away from the body because its fleshy materiality is a reminder of his own mortality, and of the carnal horrors that lie beneath his skin. His black clothing, covering all of his body save for the face and the hands, reinforces the contrast between him and the naked corpse on his dissecting table. Scarpetta, on the other hand, seems largely untroubled by abjection because she does not see on her autopsy table

---

[27] K. Howell, 'The suspicious figure of the female forensic pathologist investigator in crime fiction', *M/C Journal*, 15.1, (2012). https://doi.org/10.5204/mcj.454

[28] J. Kristeva, *The Powers of Horror: An Essay on Abjection*, trans. L. S. Roudiez (Columbia University Press, 1984), p. 3

the viscera that vexes the border between being and not being, but rather the pieces of a puzzle that she can put together in order to animate the victim's story.

By placing a woman in the dissecting room, Cornwell creates a very different image from that of 'The Anatomy Lesson' and renegotiates the value of the medical gaze, focusing not only on the humanity of the dead body but also on its symbolic resurrection through the recovery of the secrets that are imprinted upon it and hidden inside it. In *The Body Emblazoned* (1995), Jonathan Sawday explores the histories and cultures of dissection at length, arguing that the Renaissance marked a shift in perceptions of the nature and value of the human body, and that these were aided by advances in dissection. As Michal Kobialka puts it, Sawday's study marked a move from 'logocentric towards corporeal investigations' in Renaissance studies,[29] and a similar shift can be seen in crime fiction from the logocentric investigations of Auguste Dupin to the corporeal ones of Scarpetta and her fictional peers. A shift away from logocentric investigation can be seen in the forensic novel's privileging of material evidence, but the gaze that the female medical examiner brings to the body is unlike that of her male Renaissance predecessors. Gill Plain has argued that, in crime fiction, the victim's body is 'carried off in the opening pages and safely translated into symbol' while 'the material reality of the corpse decomposes beneath their narrative indifference.' In a footnote, she acknowledges that Cornwell 'brings the body centre stage', but notes that 'the body is dehumanised' because it is 'reduced to a series of component parts'.[30] Nicole Kenley also focuses on the importance of the body as a site of fact and knowledge, arguing that Cornwell 'turns body into data ... For Scarpetta, the body equals evidence and evidence equals fact'.[31] Both readings, however, overlook the humanity and compassion that Scarpetta brings to her work – qualities that mark her out as an outsider in a male-dominated environment. In *Point of Origin*, FBI profiler Benton Wesley tells Scarpetta 'I know all the same details you do', thereby supporting Plain's view that in this type of novel the victim's bodily integrity is 'violated by the detective' who is interested in the body as a series of facts.[32] Scarpetta, however, offers a reply that challenges this view: 'You don't put your hands inside their ruined bodies and touch and measure wounds. ... you don't hear them speak after they're dead. You don't see the faces of loved ones

[29] M. Kobialka, 'Delirium of the flesh: "All the dead voices" in the space of the now', in M. Bleeker (ed.), *Anatomy Live: Performance and the Operating Theatre* (Amsterdam University Press, 2008), p. 224

[30] G. Plain, *Twentieth-Century Crime Fiction: Gender, Sexuality and the Body* (Edinburgh: Edinburgh University Press, 2001), pp. 12, 16

[31] N. Kenley, 'Global crime, forensic detective fiction, and the continuum of containment', *Canadian Review of Comparative Literature*, 46 (2019), 96–114 (98)

[32] Plain, *Twentieth-Century Crime Fiction*, p. 16

waiting inside my poor, plain lobby to hear heartless, unspeakable news. . . . you spend more time with the killers than with those they ripped from life.'[33] It is hard to reconcile these words with Plain's argument that the 'pathologist's proximity to the body does not in itself challenge the genre's traditional distance from the corpse', and it is equally hard to recognise in this description Vanacker's view of Scarpetta as a masculinist 'dealer in death.'[34] Vanacker overlooks many of Scarpetta's qualities that align her more closely with the role of the life-giver and the care-giver than they do with the male hero of the crime novel. To understand this further, we need to take a closer look at how female bodies are depicted through the examiner's gaze.

The first example of sustained engagement with the body of a dead female in crime fiction can be found in Poe. 'The Mystery of Marie Rogêt' is the second of the three Dupin stories, and, in many ways, the oddest. Based on a true story and famously unsolved by the genius detective, the tale also lacks narrative drive and the intricate plotting that made the other Dupin stories a success. What is of interest and relevance to the modern forensic novel, though, is the story's focus on the female victim's body. Published just a year before 'The Philosophy of Composition', where Poe famously claimed that the death of a beautiful woman is the most poetic subject in the word, the story contains a detailed description of the dead woman's body that is worth quoting at length:

> The face was suffused with dark blood, some of which issued from the mouth. No foam was seen, as in the case of the merely drowned. There was no discoloration in the cellular tissue. About the throat were bruises and impressions of fingers. The arms were bent over on the chest and were rigid. The right hand was clenched; the left partially open. On the left wrist were two circular excoriations, apparently the effect of ropes, or of a rope in more than one volution. A part of the right wrist, also, was much chafed, as well as the back throughout its extent, but more especially at the shoulder-blades. In bringing the body to the shore the fishermen had attached to it a rope; but none of the excoriations had been effected by this. The flesh of the neck was much swollen. There were no cuts apparent, or bruises which appeared the effect of blows. A piece of lace was found tied so tightly around the neck as to be hidden from sight; it was completely buried in the flesh, and was fastened by a knot which lay just under the left ear. This alone would have sufficed to produce death. The medical testimony spoke confidently of the virtuous character of the deceased. She had been subjected, it said, to brutal violence. The corpse was in such condition when found, that there could have been no difficulty in its recognition by friends.

---

[33] P. Cornwell, *Point of Origin* (London: Warner, 1998), p. 15

[34] Plain, *Twentieth-Century Crime Fiction*, p. 16; and Vanacker, *Criminal Proceedings*, p. 66

> The dress was much torn and otherwise disordered. In the outer garment,
> a slip, about a foot wide, had been torn upward from the bottom hem to the
> waist, but not torn off.[35]

The description is notable not only for its focus on forensic detail but also for the symbolic power of the forensic gaze. The narrator begins by describing her face, the seat of her beauty and strongest marker of her identity as a beautiful dead woman. The gaze then moves downwards to the throat, the arms and the wrists, and back to the neck. The gaze is then withheld: rather than moving on to the lower part of the body, the narrator draws a metaphorical veil over the victim's nether regions and assures us instead that the deceased was of 'virtuous character'. The conflation of rape with loss of virtue is greatly troubling to a modern audience, and yet, as Cornwell and other authors of the twentieth and twenty-first centuries have shown, the underlying attitudes to the victims of sexual violence may not have evolved as much as we would like to believe. The paragraph that follows takes the gaze down to the end of the victim's long garments and engages in a form of narrative striptease that moves the layers upwards from the feet towards the waist, and inwards from the outside in, closer to those parts of the female anatomy that would confirm or betray her 'virtue'. The narrative hesitation belongs both to the narrator and to the collective of the judicial and medical gaze; by avoiding the direct depiction of the victim's private parts, the narrator seemingly attempts to preserve and protect her 'virtue' even as he exposes the underlying reality of victim-blaming. Earlier in the story, the narrator had already noted that '[t]he atrocity of this murder (for it was at once evident that murder had been committed), the youth and beauty of the victim, and, above all, her previous notoriety, conspired to produce intense excitement in the minds of the sensitive Parisians.'[36] A beautiful and notorious woman is an object of suspicion, and the withholding of the description of the body from the waist down is an attempt to preserve a 'virtue' which, by that society's standards, was already lost or surrendered. Nearly a century and a half later, Cornwell would make the link between the female victim's body and questions of morality and virtue much more explicit. In the opening pages of the first Scarpetta novel, the narrator muses: 'The dead are defenseless ... I did what I could to preserve the dignity of the victims'[37] – a declaration that acknowledges the potential for violation inherent in her examinations.

Scarpetta's examination of Lori Petersen's body is reminiscent of Poe's description in the way that the gaze moves: 'her face was grotesque, swollen beyond recognition ... her straw-blonde hair was in disarray ... she was

---

[35] Poe, 'The Mystery of Marie Rogêt', in *The Complete Tales*, pp. 174–5.   [36] Ibid., p. 171.
[37] Cornwell, *Postmortem*, pp. 10–11.

moderately tall'.[38] The gaze starts with the face, focuses on the neck and hair, and then zooms out to give an estimate of the victim's height. She then also draws a veil over the realities and indignities of taking the body's temperature, and concludes with a note of 'the musky smell, the patches of residue, transparent and dried like glue, on the upper front and back of her legs.'[39] The location of the seminal fluid externally on the legs spares the victim a further violation, with both Cornwell and Scarpetta preserving a little of Lori Petersen's dignity, or what Poe and his narrator would have thought of as her virtue. Scarpetta also refrains from naming the glue-like substance while she is describing the body. It is only in the next paragraph that she names the substance as semen, and by then she has moved away from a description of the body to an explanation of the perpetrator's status as a non-secreter. Safer now, away from the female body and firmly on medical and scientific ground, Scarpetta can finally name semen and discuss its significance in 'DNA profiling, newly introduced and potentially significant enough to identify an assailant to the exclusion of all other human beings'.[40] Scarpetta later conducts a fuller examination of the victim, narrated once again without much emphasis on the sexual nature of the crime. At the end of the process, she finds herself 'trying to dictate Lori Petersen's autopsy report. For some reason, I couldn't say anything, couldn't bear to hear the words out loud. It began to dawn on me that no one should hear these words.'[41] The tension between the need to document the process of the post-mortem and the need to minimise the violence by not articulating it is significant in this scene. It helps to depict Scarpetta as a caring physician who wants to shield others from the gruesome realities of death and murder, but it also points to another truth. Forensic crime novels such as Cornwell's speak of the need to protect the victims, while they also literally articulate the violence that they condemn: each Scarpetta story is a saying-out-loud of the violence that dehumanises her victims. This contradiction continues to haunt the forensic crime novel, and has led to initiatives such as the short-lived Staunch Book prize, whose aim was to promote crime fiction 'in which no woman is beaten, stalked, sexually exploited, raped or murdered'.[42]

The need to balance representations of gendered violence is also evident in the works of Kathy Reichs. Her 1997 debut, *Déjà Dead*, introduced Temperance Brennan, who shares with Scarpetta a sense of compassion for the female victims of violence, and a mixture of strength and expertise as a professional and vulnerability and fear as a woman. Early on in her narrative Brennan, another first-person narrator, describes the body of Chantal Trottier. She too

---

[38] Ibid., p. 15.   [39] Ibid., p. 16.   [40] Ibid.   [41] Ibid., p. 36.
[42] About: Staunch Book Prize (http://staunchbookprize.com/about-2/).

begins with the head, the face, and the hair, moving to the trunk and then down to the waist. Like her predecessors, she then goes on to draw a veil over the lower half of the body, noting only the position of the legs and the moving detail of the toenails 'painted a soft pink'.[43] What are we to make of the forensic novel's dual emphasis on the female victim and the female investigator, where the latter needs both to uncover the crime but also to conceal some of its horrors? Brennan may be protecting her victim's modesty and dignity, but the novel as a whole derives a lot of its appeal from the depiction of gruesome violence. One way of reconciling the twin impulses involves an understanding of the act of reading as analogous to the pathologist's work. Our pleasure derives not from the portrayal of violence, but rather from the ways in which the investigation makes the violence legible, and thus contains its horror. The bodies that Scarpetta, Brennan, and their peers examine are also bodies that are being read, and it is in the act of interpretative reading that reader and investigator converge. Katharine and Lee Horsley note that Scarpetta 'claims that what her role gives her is privileged access to "the real" as it is embodied in the torn and open body'. They go on to argue that by using a forensic pathologist as her protagonist,

> Cornwell makes possible a more 'corporeally sophisticated' reading of the corpse-as-text, using the body as the evidentiary basis for readings of the crime. But more than that, she creates a central intelligence which is empowered to speak directly about the body as witness to truth. Scarpetta's unmediated access to the traumatised corpse endows her with the almost unchallengeable authority that comes with intimate knowledge of the unbearable and unthinkable; she gives voice to what would otherwise remain simply 'unspeakable'.[44]

Brennan plays a similar role in Reichs's series. In *Déjà Dead*, the narrative opens with Brennan not thinking about 'the man who'd blown himself up'. 'Earlier I had', she explains, but now 'I was putting him together.'[45] To put the body together is to render it legible, to recover its story. For her next task, Brennan needs to reassemble a skeleton from remains found in separate plastic bags. She goes about it in a systematic fashion, assembling and labelling with machine-like efficiency, but has to conclude her report by noting that the name of the deceased is unknown: 'Number it. Photograph it. Take samples. Tag the toe. While I am an active participant, I can never accept the impersonality of the system. It is like looting on the most personal level. At least I would give this

[43] K. Reichs, *Déjà Dead* (London: Arrow Books, 1997), p. 46.
[44] K. and L. Horlsey, 'Body language: Reading the corpse in forensic crime fiction', *Paradoxa*, 20 (2006), 1–30 (p. 1).
[45] Reichs, *Déjà Dead*, p. 1.

victim a name. Death in anonymity would not be added to the list of violations he or she would suffer.'[46] Like Scarpetta, Brennan does not confront the abject when she gazes at her victim's remains. Instead, she sees a post-mortem human with an identity and a story to tell. In addition, by virtue of being first-person narrators, both Brennan and Scarpetta embody the authority conferred upon them: they tell the stories of the dead.

The idea of the corpse as text is central to a lot of forensically themed crime fiction, but in novels that feature female investigators solving crimes against female bodies the corpse, and the text, have a level of specificity that needs to be examined more closely. If we think of Sherlock Holmes and his crime-solving methods, what we see is a mastery of science and a dazzling ability to read crime scenes through the application of observation, logical deduction, and scientific knowledge. The process of deduction is one that is suppressed in forensic crime fiction that features female medical examiners. It is, rather, the material evidence of the body that is highlighted; whereas Holmes arrives at the truth by bringing together fragments that do not cohere in anyone else's mind, Scarpetta and her peers recover a narrative that already exists, imprinted on the traumatised body and less in need of a unifying intellect. Holmes may be more of a Barthesian reader, one able to create meaning out of fragments that have been chosen by him and that have not been designed by a controlling intelligence (within the fictional world, that is). Scarpetta, Brennan, and their peers, on the other hand, are on a quest to uncover and discover the story of the crime, authored by the perpetrator and concealed within the body. Subsequently, part of our enjoyment of this type of crime fiction derives from the fact that the answers will be authoritative, definitive, and restorative: the investigation will *recover* rather than *discover*. The recovery of a story brings with it consolation; it points to a stable, accessible reality that can be arrived at through the application of science. Making figurative use of Locard's principle that every contact leaves a trace, these novels suggest that the traces can lead to recovery in both senses of the word: recovery of the story of the crime, and recovery of a society after the excision of evil. Alongside the forensic novel's privileging of the body and the medical gaze, though, a darker truth persists. A lot of forensic fiction does little to examine the social causes of crime, nor does it highlight the mundane reality that women are usually killed by their partners and not by deranged serial killers. The fictional consolation that comes with scientific truth and knowledge thus conceals the reality of crime and thereby gives solace that is partially false.

---

[46] Ibid., p. 20.

Rose Lucas asks why tales of gruesome murder are so popular: 'on one level, I am sickened by their stories of demented or malicious violence, by the jaundiced view of society and its institutions ... and in particular by their graphic descriptions of cruel violations inflicted upon human bodies. But I turn away even as I look, needing to *know*.'[47] The simultaneous attraction and revulsion that is felt by the reader of forensic crime fiction is best understood with the aid of Julia Kristeva's concept of abjection. As Lucas observes, 'Cornwell's novels activate the reader's concerns about a wide variety of threats to their sense of an intact self, both corporeally and socially.'[48] The sense of an intact self, according to Kristeva, comes from a rejection of the abject: the leaking parts of the body, the blood and waste products contained within, threaten the sense of an intact self. Lucas astutely links the concept of interiority with the images of viscera: 'we have tended to read interiority as synonymous with a psychological, spiritual, or intellectual dimension',[49] she notes, but we do this at the expense of acknowledging the physical reality of our interiority. The forensic pathologist offers solace and reconciliation: by examining the literal interior of the deceased, she restores the victim's interiority by conferring an identity upon the body, and by telling the story of how the body came to be. Katharine and Lee Horsley also see this reconciliation as the pathologist's function within the text:

> The forensic pathologist engaged in reconstructing the victim's suffering and identity must (for the narrative to move towards closure) bring the abject back within the symbolic order. The resolution of the crime novel most often makes instrumental and admonitory use of its grim material, evoking disgust with the crime committed, registering breakdowns of order which might be remediable – that require action, if only condemnation. To this end, the forensic pathologist has in effect to reconstitute a narrative by reassembling the fragmented body parts – recontaining the horror, reconstructing the abject body, negotiating amongst different possible scriptings of the victim's fate, reincorporating the body within a narrative structure that will rescue it from abjection.[50]

This rescuing from abjection is a hallmark of the female protagonist in this type of crime fiction, and one way in which we can understand it is by considering the history of traditionally female roles concerning the tending of the newly born and the newly dead. Both babies and newly dead people occupy that liminal space that Kristeva associates with abjection; they are bodies without

---

[47] R. Lucas, 'Anxiety and its antidotes: Patricia Cornwell and the forensic body', *Literature Interpretation Theory*, 15.2 (2010), 207–22 (p. 210).

[48] Ibid., 215.   [49] Ibid., 219.

[50] K. and L. Horsley, 'Body language: Reading the corpse in forensic crime fiction', 20.

selves. And both are cared for by women, babies most obviously by the mother or the wet nurse, but also the dead as their bodies are prepared for internment or cremation. Therefore, whereas medical examiners would have been over-whelmingly male when Cornwell started the Scarpetta series, as they had been through the ages, the female medical examiner appears to have resonated in ways that become legible once we examine the unacknowledged roles that women have played in the invisible space of domestic environments.

One of the features of the Scarpetta novels is the protagonist's combination of strength and vulnerability. Hammett used the dream sequence as a device to depict the Continental Op's hidden fears and insecurities, while Chandler made Marlowe a man with no personal life and not much to call home. The few glimpses into his feelings were always fleeting, and always rendered in his arch, highly stylised manner that sought to question or undermine the very thing he was trying to express. Scarpetta, by contrast, is honest about her feelings and often discusses her fears, insecurities, and the situations that make her uncom-fortable. One of the best examples of how Cornwell marries strength and vulnerability in her protagonist can be found in *Body of Evidence*. At the end of chapter 8, at home at night, Scarpetta plays a message left on her answer-phone by an old flame, and then slumps against her pillows and cries. The next morning, as a new chapter begins, she is depicted making a Y incision on a victim's body and lifting out the internal organs. The literal and metaphorical depictions of having a broken heart and a heart lifted out of the ribcage are deftly brought together to show how the female investigator can be both strong and vulnerable. In those scenes, and throughout the series, Scarpetta is aware of, and articulate about, her need at times to perform and at times to embody different identities. Brennan is equally comfortable exposing her vulnerability to the reader. As with Cornwell, Reichs counterbalances this vulnerability with a sense of authority that comes with the protagonist's scientific background, and especially through depictions of the imparting of knowledge from female to male.

In *Body of Evidence*, Scarpetta explains the concept of chirality to Marino in a scene that, like all scenes of its kind, accomplishes two things: it saves the author from the danger of exposition, and at the same time it asserts the female's mastery and her sense of superiority over her physically stronger and more respected male colleagues. Scarpetta may be unable to fend off an attacker, but she can describe the difference between dextromethorphan and levomethorphan in ways that the detective confesses '[d]on't mean a damn thing' to him.[51] Similarly, when Brennan learns that 'Claudel doesn't put much stock in this

---

[51] Cornwell, *Body of Evidence*, p. 236.

cut-mark business', believing that 'a saw's a saw',[52] she launches into an eight-page lecture that showcases her specialist knowledge of different types of saw and the different marks they leave on bones. Her interlocutor becomes more and more interested in her science, and convinced of her knowledge and expertise. By the end of the sequence, she has gained an ally whose help she enlists in fighting against Claudel's resistance to her theories. In *Body of Evidence*, Scarpetta is depicted having a conversation with a witness who becomes impatient with her unwillingness to discuss intuitive rather than empirical knowledge. 'You're being the scientist', he says in an accusatory tone. 'I am a scientist', comes her confident reply,[53] reminding her interlocutor that her professional identity should not be separated from her character. Yet privately, when she is speaking to the reader rather than the character who sought her out, she also confesses that she was 'sitting calmly, my powers of imagination switched off, the scientist, the clinician deliberately donned like a suit of clothes'.[54] Cornwell engages in a complex negotiation between performance and embodiment throughout the series, drawing attention to the way in which Scarpetta is both an astute observer of her working environment and a woman who is highly aware of the male gaze and the scrutiny it brings upon her.

Kathy Reichs and Tess Gerritsen in the US, and Val McDermid in the UK, have followed in Cornwell's footsteps and added significant new elements to the sub-genre, especially in their focus on female identities, and they have all enlisted the application of forensic science to help them achieve that. Scarpetta is depicted, and sees herself, as a lone warrior fighting to bring justice and retore humanity to the violated female body. Surrounded by misogynists and people suspicious of her authority, she undertakes this work alone. Therefore, even though she solves the crime, the early novels do not suggest a viable way for her to exist as a female investigator in her world. That may explain why her niece Lucy grows older at a faster rate than Scarpetta does throughout the series. The introduction of another female character, and one who like Scarpetta represents a rejection of traditional female roles, allows the author to create alternative female spaces and bonds that challenge the hetero-normativity of the crime novel. Gerritsen similarly started with Jane Rizzoli but not Maura Isles. In *The Surgeon*, the first novel of the series, Rizzoli is seen through a male detective's eyes as 'a small and square-jawed woman' whose face 'seemed to be all hard angles ... She was the only woman in the homicide unit, and already there had been problems between her and another detective, charges of sexual harassment, countercharges of unrelenting bitchiness.'[55]

---

[52] Reichs, *Déjà Dead*, p. 156.   [53] Cornwell, *Body of Evidence*, p. 218.   [54] Ibid., p. 219.
[55] T. Gerritsen, *The Surgeon* (London: Ballantine Books, 2001), p. 12.

Rizzoli thus both lacks conventional feminine attributes and is the recipient of sexist attitude and behaviours. Her subsequent partnership with Maura Isles enables Gerritsen to highlight contrasting and complementary qualities in the two female professionals that move beyond the early stereotypical images of *The Surgeon*. McDermid places a lot of value on networks of female friendship and solidarity. In our interview (see Appendix 2), she spoke of how she was influenced by Sara Paretsky and Sue Grafton, noting that she saw in their work new possibilities for the crime novel, but also an absence of extensive female networks that were important both to her own conception of female solidarity and to her lived experience.

McDermid is different from Reichs, Cornwell, and Gerritsen for two main reasons. She writes a number of series featuring different investigators, and the series are equally successful, so it is hard to identify one of them as the dominant work and therefore to draw conclusions about the type of investigator she favours in her writing. The novels highlight different investigative methods and different types of investigator. The investigative process is often depicted as collaborative and distributed, moving the genre away from its emphasis on the lone heroic investigator. Notably, none of her female protagonists are medical experts. Instead of taking us to the autopsy table, McDermid often shows her investigators seeking the expertise of others in order to piece together the evidence that solves the case. The absence of a female medical expert allows McDermid to avoid many of the criticisms levelled at the other authors, whose medical experts risk imposing a totalising gaze on the world around them. Her fictional worlds are more nuanced, and more concerned with the social causes of crime, for example. They are also interested in the science of things as much as the science of the body, and therefore showcase a wealth of forensic evidence that is not as focused on the female corpse as it is in the other authors' corpus. Through a long and fruitful association with Professor Dame Sue Black and Professor Niamh Nic Daeid (formerly and currently of the University of Dundee, Scotland, respectively), McDermid has been able to use a whole range of forensic detail with authority and credibility. As she explained, reaching out to the experts has also given her an advantage by allowing her to include in her novels cutting-edge forensic science before it becomes available to other writers or known to the public. However, the application of forensic science never becomes an end in itself in McDermid's fiction. Her novels contain a wealth of forensic detail, and all the plot twists and cliff hangers we expect of the genre, but they are also imbued with a sensibility that makes us read for character, and a sense of place that is as seductive as the plot. When asked whether a novelist can have too much forensic detail in their books, she replied:

I think you have to be careful not to fall in love with the technology. It's very seductive, but you put in what you have to put in. I try to avoid too detailed explanations because that's dull; it's about writing enough to convey the 'wow' factor, but not necessarily having to put in all the details of the science. And sometimes you read a novel where the author does not follow this advice and your eyes glaze over.

Section 2 takes a closer look at the science of forensic crime fiction, guided by the comments made by Val McDermid and Professor Niamh Nic Daeid in the interviews that were conducted for this Element. Fictionalised versions of Professor Nic Daeid can be found in McDermid's fiction, where the author takes great care to portray science and scientists in ways that are accurate and not sensationalised. The insights that these two professionals offer in the interviews have been important in shaping the argument that follows.

2 The Limits of Science

Why are readers fascinated by forensic science? How can critics explain the immense popularity of blockbuster novels and TV shows that depict the application of science in the solving of crime? The origins of the crime genre contain clues that can help to answer these questions. The material evidence in the Rue Morgue, for example, was not only novel, but also extensive, detailed, and conclusive. Whereas the witnesses who heard the confrontation in the apartment described the 'foreign' voice as belonging to a language they didn't speak, the strands of hair, broken furniture, and blood-smeared razor told a story that was much more reliable and objective than that of the human witnesses. Conversely, in 'The Purloined Letter', material evidence did nothing to solve the case. Poe delighted in proving that the application of science and technology cannot replace truths that are arrived at through empathy and the imagination: Dupin found the letter not by conducting a forensic search, but more simply by asking himself where he might have hidden it had he been Minister D. The mistrust of the scientific method, then, is what solved this case. Andrea Goulet argues that the hardboiled novel also displays a mistrust of science and notes, for example, that 'Dashiell Hammett's hardboiled private eyes were renouncing forensic technologies like fingerprinting as "forms of quackery"'.[56] Both Dupin and the hardboiled private eyes sought to distance themselves from official methods of investigation, and in both cases their mistrust reflected a wider concern with the limits of epistemological certainty as well as with organised law enforcement. Alongside the mistrust of science, Dupin exhibited a mistrust of the police

---

[56] A. Goulet, 'Crime fiction and modern science', in Janice Allan, Jesper Gulddal, Stewart King, and Andrew Pepper (eds.), *The Routledge Companion to Crime Fiction* (London: Routledge, 2020), pp. 291–300 (p. 295).

force as the embodiment of both rationality and authority. The Parisian police, he tells the narrator, 'are exceedingly able *in their way*. They are persevering, ingenious, cunning, and thoroughly versed in *the knowledge which their duties seem chiefly to demand*.' However, they err 'by being too deep or too shallow for the matter in hand'.[57] His pointed remarks barely disguise the contempt he feels for a professional body that can only solve crime through the application of a narrow body of knowledge and a prescribed set of methodologies. With Dupin, Poe created a type that was taken up by Arthur Conan Doyle and developed by many subsequent crime writers: the charismatic amateur detective or professional private investigator who outsmarts the police. The tension between amateur and professional, and between scientific method and imagination, is both appealing and unsettling.

If science and the police cannot be trusted to solve crime, how can the crime story restore us to the state of innocence that W. H. Auden postulates in 'The Guilty Vicarage'?[58] Much of forensic fiction appears to resolve this tension. The application of science is depicted as infallible, and therefore capable of overriding any corruption that might exist in the system. Cops may be bent and liable to suppressing the truth, for example, but the evidence never lies. In this way, forensic crime fiction breaks the mould of other types of crime writing by suggesting that there are certainties in the world, and evidence that is objective, stable, and reliable. Sherlock Holmes is perhaps the most perfect embodiment of this belief: his mastery of material evidence allows him to make pronouncements that leave no room for doubt or misinterpretation. That this evidence is often either not visible to the naked eye or overlooked by other observers adds to the appeal: it seems miraculous that things that the human eye cannot see or perceive can provide evidence that uncovers crime. Conan Doyle used Dr Watson both to heighten and to mock this effect: Watson is often dazzled by Holmes's extraordinary conclusions, but appears disappointed when Holmes explains the evidence that led to his discoveries. Conan Doyle was thereby drawing attention to the fact that material evidence need not be literally invisible to be extraordinary; it is the controlling intellect of the investigator that makes meaning out of the evidence. This complex relationship between the seen and the unseen was also of interest to Poe; Dupin famously gives the example of the map game, where skilled players can look closely to find the placenames with the tiniest print, when the real challenge is to find the large letters that stretch across the map.[59]

---

[57] Poe, 'The Purloined Letter', pp. 214–15 (emphasis added).

[58] W. H. Auden, 'The Guilty Vicarage', in *The Dyer's Hand and Other Essays* (London: Faber and Faber, 1975), pp. 146–58.

[59] Poe, 'The Purloined Letter', p. 219.

The meaning-making that forensic science enables within forensic crime narratives both mirrors and queries the meaning-making inherent in the reading of the stories themselves. Forensic scientists are the privileged readers of clues, gathering the evidence and helping to weave a story out of it. The pleasure of reading crime fiction often derives from that same impulse to gather, order, and interpret clues. In traditional crime fiction, the author can frustrate the reader's interpretative impulse by withholding some evidence, by planting false clues, or by sustaining until late in the narrative the possibility of multiple outcomes. The use of forensic science creates new challenges in this relationship between reader and text. Because the reader is not normally equipped to assess or interpret the value and significance of scientific evidence, the interpretative onus is passed on to the forensic scientist in the text. This alters the dynamics of interpretation and opens up new ways of engaging with material evidence. One key difference between the forensic crime novel and its television counterpart, for example, is that the latter can render microscopic evidence visible. Many forensic-themed TV shows use special effects to show the viewer what the evidence looks like under a microscope, and this alters our relationship with the fiction. In the forensic crime novel, the evidence remains invisible, and it is the scientist who needs to explain it to the reader, the explanation often conveyed in scenes of dialogue with the investigating police officers. That confers authority to the scientist in a way that the TV show doesn't: on TV, we see the evidence that the scientist sees, and that diminishes their achievement. Just as Watson laughs when he is presented with the evidence that Holmes used to reach his seemingly impossible conclusions, so we viewers feel we can interpret the evidence without the controlling intellect of the scientist. The visualisation of invisible evidence explains much of the appeal of the genre on TV: the literalisation of material that would otherwise remain inaccessible helps to build a narrative of trust in material evidence: it is easier for us to dismiss things we cannot see or comprehend, but harder to do so when we see them magnified on our screens. In this way, TV shows present a view of scientific and material evidence as stable and incontrovertible, whereas crime fiction presents a more complex picture.

One of the ways in which both TV shows and novels differ from real life is that, in real life, forensic science is often used as supporting evidence in court, rather than driving the investigation. It is often more mundane things to do with a person's movements, their associates, and their familial relationships that help to solve crime. In addition, forensic evidence is not always objective and conclusive – and nor is it always science, as Professor Niamh Nic Daeid notes (see Appendix 1). She explains that forensic evidence

is hardly ever the 'smoking gun' that we associate with fictional investigations, and gives the examples of clothing fibres and DNA samples,
pointing out that a DNA sample may contain several profiles because the
detection is so sensitive compared to when DNA was first used in the
1980s:

> if we get multiple DNA profiles and our challenge is trying to sort them out,
> the person of interest's DNA might be in that mixture, but that does not
> necessarily imply that person is responsible for the alleged crime, only that
> their DNA might be present. . . . Often we deal with source level propositions:
> does that DNA profile come from this individual? Or does that fibre come
> from this jumper? And we're not always able to answer that question because
> we don't know how many similar jumpers there may be or the DNA profile
> may be difficult to interpret.[60]

The use of scientific evidence as 'corroboration of a set of potential activities'
contains a degree of uncertainty that forensic crime fiction would find intoler-
able, because the genre relies on the strength of scientific fact and equates
scientific knowledge with authority. Professor Nic Daeid explains that not
everything that we consider to be forensic science is actually science at all:
'Other areas of forensic evidence are not objective. They are almost entirely
subjective, such as the comparison of fingerprints and the linkage of bullets to
guns. The comparison of tool marks, handwriting, footwear marks – all of those
are almost wholly subjective analysis.'

Brennan's long treatise on the different types of saw marks is therefore less
scientific than the narrative would have us believe, but within the logic of the
novel, and within its generic parameters, the reader accepts it as evidence of
the scientist's mastery of her field. In court, a forensic scientist is called upon
to explain very complex data and processes in ways that are not compatible
with the popular perception that the evidence never lies. To learn that there is
a large element of subjectivity is to arrive at an understanding of the uses and
applications of forensic analysis that forensic crime fiction has not prepared us
for at all. If forensic science is less central to the solving of crime than fiction
would have us believe, and if the science depicted in the fiction is more
reliable than its equivalent in real life, what, then, is the relationship between
forensic science in the real world and forensic science as depicted in fiction?
To consider that question, we need to consider the concept of realism. In
'Reading *The Operation*', Catherine Belling makes an important distinction
between the term 'realism' as used in everyday contexts and its use in literary

---

[60] See Appendix 1 for full interview. Further references to this interview also taken from
Appendix 1.

analysis. In a non-literary context, realism often means an accurate representation of external reality. In literary criticism, though, it can have a more
specific meaning that does not ask the represented to be true to an external
referent, but rather to be true within the logic of this and other fictional
worlds.[61] Kerstin Bergman acknowledges the difference between the two by
explaining how 'in the following discussion regarding how authors or produ-
cers attempt to make things appear true, the reference is to how their fictional
works portray something as accurate and believable *within the context of the
fictional world*'.[62] Science is used with some poetic licence by crime novelists
in order to make things appear true within a fictional world, with the ultimate
aim of providing consolatory narratives in which knowledge and empirical
evidence defeat the irrational forces of evil. Realism does not always denote
the accurate representation of reality. It can also mean the believable, sustained application of literary convention across a fiction, but forensic crime
novels can only make limited use of this distinction. A novelist may be able to
shorten a sequence and expedite the publication of test results, for example, or
they might make the results of a test seem more conclusive, but they do not use
imaginary or incorrect forensic science, even if that science could be made
plausible and consistent. For many, readerly pleasure is derived from learning
about forensic science through the novels, and then researching it further in
the increasing corpus of non-fictional works on the subject. Asked whether she
would consider inventing a fictional piece of forensic evidence, Val
McDermid replied no. The science itself, she argued, moves so fast that there's
hardly any need to invent any of it. Further, she explained that getting the
science right adds authority to all other aspects of the novel, helping her to
create a complete and engaging fictional world. She did acknowledge, however, that sometimes the writer has to take liberties, altering the timescale of
the investigation for the sake of narrative propulsion, or not revealing scientific information that could fall into the wrong hands, such as when describing
the making of a bomb.

The forensic novel needs to be as true to life as is possible, but often it is true
to what we believe to be true life because we know it from fiction. Suzanne Bell
calls this a 'chicken or egg' situation:

> Movies such as *The Silence of the Lambs*, *The Bone Collector*, and *Kiss the
> Girls* (all based on best-selling novels) blithely sidestep the realities of
> forensic psychiatry, forensic investigation, and forensic psychology in the
> name of fictional license. This is not a crime (pun intended); all are

---

[61] C. Belling, 'Reading *The Operation*: Television, realism, and the possession of medical
knowledge.' *Literature and Medicine*, 17.1 (1998), 1–23 (2).
[62] Bergman, 'Fictional death and scientific truth', p. 89 (emphasis added).

marketed as fiction. The danger is that the audience, bombarded with the triumphs of forensic fiction, grows to expect the same feats from the real thing.[63]

The notion that fictional forensic science is more widely understood than its real-life equivalent has led to speculation that juries are now afflicted by 'the *CSI* effect': they demand evidence that either does not exist, or that is too costly or unnecessary to be used in court. It is not certain whether the *CSI* effect actually exists, but the concept is useful in helping us to understand the crime reader's demand that the work be believable, accurate, and realistic. How we arrive at these valuations is a complex issue. We judge the realism of the investigation with reference to other fictional investigations, for example, but in so doing we are not certain of their factual accuracy. The forensic crime novel exposes our willingness to accept sustained fictions as truths, and this can be dangerous because sustained fictions can easily replace realities. In the absence of access to detailed and specialist scientific knowledge, readers can rely on knowledge gleaned from reading forensic crime novels. We 'know' how DNA evidence can lead to a killer, even if we do not really appreciate either the complexities of interpreting DNA evidence or the ease with which such evidence can transfer across surfaces. To believe that the sustained realism of the fictional world is equivalent to, or coincident with, scientific knowledge is a dangerous notion. The extensive use of misinformation during the Covid-19 pandemic, for example, has made this observation painfully clear. Scientific, pseudo-scientific, and anti-scientific narratives all competed for attention and dominance, with little attempt to question how each one was created or legitimised. If enough conspiracy theorists have the same theory of how a vaccine may harm you, then it becomes easy to treat their collectively sustained fiction as evidence.

Despite not always having the means to judge the accuracy and reliability of forensic science in fiction, readers demand believable science and originality, forcing authors to continue to research and probe the limits of science and technology. In the UK, Lin Anderson started her crime writing career by taking a course in forensic science at the University of Glasgow in order to be able to write confidently in the sub-genre. In her 2018 novel, *Sins of the Dead*, her protagonist, forensic scientist Rhona MacLeod, is depicted teaching forensic science at the University of Glasgow to an audience not unlike the one that Anderson herself was part of. In the real world, the author used the university course to learn more about crime-solving, but in the fictional world it is the criminal who attends the course, in the hope of defeating the ends of justice by applying the very knowledge that is supposed to

---

[63] S. Bell, *Crime and Circumstance: Investigating the History of Forensic Science* (Westport, CT: Praeger, 2008), pp. 13–14.

help combat or solve crime. Val McDermid doesn't just seek the expertise of forensic scientists; she often portrays them sympathetically in her fiction, in a way that is more nuanced than the heroic scientist stereotype created by many of her peers. The legitimation of science needs two main ingredients: a solid basis in truth and reality, and a sympathetic fictional scientist. The former is achieved through extensive research on the part of the author, while the latter is a function of stylistic and narrative choices such as voice and point of view. If, as Val McDermid argues, the accurate depiction of forensic science is in fact useful for legitimising other parts of the narrative, allowing the author to create authoritative and credible fictional worlds, what happens when the science is wrong?

The most famous example of erroneous science is probably Dorothy L. Sayers's *The Documents in the Case*. This extraordinary novel took great risks with form and structure, but it is mainly remembered now for a blunder. The plot hinges on the fact that a very experienced mycologist unwittingly consumed a lethal amount of poisonous mushrooms. His family and the investigators agree that he would never make such a lethal mistake, and the belief in his infallibility leads to the solution: the expert has been poisoned by a synthetic version of the naturally occurring substance. The two are indistinguishable in toxicology reports, but can be differentiated using a beam of polarised light. Sayers provided a lot of evidence, using scientist characters in the story to bring this discovery to life. Unfortunately the science itself was not sound, as some of the detail was inaccurate. Cornwell used the same concept of chirality in *Body of Evidence*, where what was believed to be cough medicine turned out to be a poisonous substance. This leads to a key question: does it matter whether the synthetic version exists, as long as the concept is scientifically sound? Bettina Wahrig offers a detailed account of the science that Sayers researched and used in the novel. She notes that 'Sayers complained that her life as a mystery writer was extremely hard because she had to perform an incredible amount of research in order to construct a plot without logical or factual mistakes.'[64] Few readers would forgive a logical mistake in a crime novel, but the poison Sayers created to serve her plot proves that scientific accuracy is also of great importance. Natalie Foster provides an equally thorough account of the scientific controversy generated by *The Documents in the Case*, and cites Sayers herself, who quipped that 'the plot was fine in the novel, but the toadstool was not'.[65] This witty remark provides

---

[64] B. Wahrig, '"Nature is lopsided": Muscarine as scientific and literary fascinosum in Dorothy L. Sayers *The Documents in the Case*', in H. Klippel et al. (eds.), *Poison and Poisoning in Science, Fiction and Cinema*, Palgrave Studies in Science and Popular Culture, pp. 57–73 (p. 69).

[65] N. Foster, 'Strong poison: Chemistry in the works of Dorothy L. Sayers', in S. M. Gerber (ed.), *Chemistry and Crime: From Sherlock Holmes to Today's Courtroom* (Washington, DC: American Chemical Society, 1983), p. 22.

a neat summary of the view that science needs to be believable rather than always accurate – though, interestingly, in this case Sayers was vindicated by later developments in science, as Foster explains. The case also serves as a reminder that science can legitimise a narrative by being accurate and up to date, but it also risks becoming obsolete as knowledge in the field moves on. I spoke to Val McDermid about this dilemma, noting how detail that seems dazzling in its newness can seem quaint a few decades later. McDermid agreed that forensic science moves very fast, but pointed out that this is a risk that any author who uses a contemporary setting has to take.

Forensic science is dazzling, but does its brilliance obscure the human factor? David A. Kirby argues that forensic science 'has changed the way entertainment professionals tell stories about law enforcement on television. What we see in contemporary television's forensic fictions is the triumph of science over humanistic modes of detection.'[66] Forensic crime novels, and especially those that feature female investigators, are different. In *Body of Evidence*, for example, Scarpetta travels to the Florida Keys in order to interview a couple who may hold the key to the fate of one of the victims. No amount of looking through powerful microscopes or dissecting bodies can compensate for the simple act of reaching out to people, explaining why their testimony matters, and appealing to their sense of justice. In the same novel, Scarpetta is visited by a young man who wants to talk to her about her investigation. 'What I have to say doesn't really belong in the category of police information', he tells her. Asked why he would think he could go to her, he replies 'as a rule, women are more intuitive, more compassionate than men'.[67] As the conversation takes a darker turn, Scarpetta switches off her powers of imagination, presenting herself as the bearer of scientific truth in order to challenge his perception of her as more intuitive, but in private she agrees. Later in the story, she has a meeting with the attorney general, who tells her that she's basing her 'theories on intuition, going on instinct. Sometimes that can be very dangerous.'[68] Scarpetta moves between two states and defends her combination of knowledge and intuition. Like Poe's Dupin, who is able to outsmart his opponent once he realises that the latter is both a mathematician and a poet, Cornwell's scientist uses a combination of different ways of knowing the world to solve crime, rather than relying on scientific knowledge alone.

Reichs's Brennan is another example. Her scientific knowledge and expertise are objective truths that cannot be challenged, and yet she has hunches and theories that put her at odds with her colleagues in law enforcement. At the start of *Déjà Dead*, returning home after work, Brennan 'began to feel the sense of

---

[66] D. A. Kirby, 'Forensic fictions: Science, television production, and modern storytelling', *Studies in History and Philosophy of Biological and Biomedical Sciences*, 44 (2013), 92–102 (p. 94).

[67] P. Cornwell, *Body of Evidence* (London: Warner, 1991), p. 217.   [68] Ibid., p. 257.

foreboding I'd experienced in the ravine. All day I'd used work to keep it at bay. I'd banished the apprehension by centering my mind fully on identifying the victim and on piecing together the late trucker. . . . now I was free to relax. To think. To worry.'[69] Premonitions of evil have no place in rational scientific thinking, and yet they are to be found in many of these novels. The forensic crime novel thrives on contradiction: It believes in science, but it also relies on the intuition, imagination, or empathy of a charismatic investigator to solve the crime. It champions the rational world of science, and yet it depicts criminality as an aberration that cannot be explained by scientific accounts. It seeks to contain and condemn violence, but it also relies on explicit and graphic depictions of it.

The various contradictions between the rational world of the forensic scientists who also use empathy, imagination, and intuition to solve crime, and the irrational world of the killer that can be contained but not explained, give the sub-genre a lot of its appeal. Crime fiction at its best does not rely on binaries: in *Red Harvest*, the Continental Op becomes blood thirsty like the natives; in *The Big Sleep*, Marlowe becomes part of the nastiness; and in numerous police procedurals the main investigator embodies the contradiction of both representing state authority and defying it in order to do their job well. The use and application of forensic science in crime fiction complicates this pattern further. As Jean Murley notes, 'the great popularity of forensics owes much to an old and powerful idea, one used in murder stories since the creation of Sherlock Holmes; that science can conquer the irrational and extract order from chaos'.[70] But the relationship between order and chaos is not a simple one. If we return to Edgar Allan Poe, we can trace the contradictory impulses of the crime story to his Dupin stories. We have seen how in his sonnet Poe accuses science of preying like a vulture on the poet's heart, destroying the mysteries of the human soul and the power of the poet's imagination. This tension between the rational world of science and the championing of the imagination is central to much writing of the Romantic period and beyond. Walt Whitman writes of his subject becoming sick and tired of hearing the learned astronomer showcase his 'charts and diagrams', leaving the lecture theatre to go and look at the stars instead.[71] Yet most Romantic poets also exhibit a great fascination with science, seen most clearly in Wordsworth and Shelley.

---

[69] Reichs, *Déjà Dead*, p. 29.

[70] J. Murley, *The Rise of True Crime: 20th-Century Murder and American Popular Culture* (Westport, CT: Praeger, 2008), p. 132.

[71] W. Whitman, 'When I Heard the Learn'd Astronomer' (1865), The Walt Whitman Archive (https://whitmanarchive.org/published/LG/1891/poems/125).

Poe used the Dupin stories as an opportunity to test the limits and the possibilities of empirical evidence and scientific enquiry without having to give up his belief in other, less-well understood powers of the human mind. J. Gerald Kennedy has made a significant contribution to our understanding of Poe's marriage of the rational and irrational impulses, in the Dupin stories and beyond: 'In a canon of fiction preponderantly devoted to terror, madness, disease, death, and revivification', he writes, 'Poe's tales of ratiocination provide a revealing counterpoint in their idealization of reason and sanity.'[72] Kennedy concludes that 'Poe finally acknowledged that ratiocination answers no questions of genuine importance, clarifies nothing about the hopes and fears of humankind.'[73] Poe is therefore dissimilar to most other writers of crime fiction, whose faith in science and logic may not be totalising or unwavering, but is certainly stronger than Poe's. Compared to Poe, Arthur Conan Doyle was a more reliable champion of science in detective fiction. Holmes is the best example of an early adopter of scientific methods and forensic investigation, and the character is fondly remembered for his powers of deduction and his extensive research into forensic evidence such as footprints and cigar ashes. Holmes makes confident pronouncements that are entirely unlike the uncertainties that Professor Nic Daeid spoke about, but his totalising vision seems harmless because the stakes are not that high in the Holmes stories. Criminality in the Holmes stories is never extreme or incomprehensible: leaving aside the fact that murder usually takes place off-stage, the stories are notable for the fact that crime has well-defined and easy to understand motives. People steal out of greed, and kill in order to inherit money or to right an old wrong. Therefore, there is no tension between the application of scientific method and the discovery of the culprit's motives. Holmes explains both the *how* and the *why*, and thus restores order and harmony to the community. This is clearly not the case in modern forensic crime fiction.

Conan Doyle used Watson as his narrator in order to create what Stephen Knight has described as a 'bridge' between the superior intellect of Holmes and the average minds of Watson and his readers.[74] This structural choice reinforces the notion that Holmes is not like other people; he is special and unique. Narrative point of view is also important in more modern forensic crime fiction, and the Scarpetta novels are a good case in point. The Scarpetta series is in fact notable for the risks that Cornwell has taken with narration. Crime series tend to follow a formula that guarantees, at the very least, stability when it comes to

---

[72] J. G. Kennedy, 'The Limits of reason: Poe's deluded detectives', *American Literature*, 47.2 (1975), 184–96 (p. 184).

[73] Ibid., p. 196.

[74] S. Knight, *Form and Ideology in Crime Fiction* (Indiana University Press, 1980), p. 43.

narrative point of view. Cornwell broke the mould with *Blow Fly* (2003), the eleventh novel in the series. After ten books narrated in the first person and the past tense, she switched to third person and the present tense. Subsequent novels in the series continued to experiment with temporal structure and point of view, and it remains to be seen whether, after *Port Mortuary* (2010), Cornwell has settled back for good into the narrative style that first made her name. There are several reasons why these choices are important. In the early days of the forensic novel, the crime author needed to convey large amounts of information about forensic science, and having an expert as first-person narrator made it easier to do that. Subsequently, as readers became more accustomed to forensic science, the stamp of authority that the narrator–expert brought to the sub-genre was less important. The present tense is a choice that seems less intuitive. With the exception of the hardboiled novel where, as Todorov has shown, the stories of crime and investigation unfold simultaneously, crime fiction normally relies on the assumption of the already-happened.[75] Narrating in the past tense therefore makes visible the fact that the crime novel is a jigsaw puzzle to be completed. The whole story precedes the narrative, and the narrative depicts the attempt to re-compose and restore the original story. The past tense in this case brings with it a sense of comfort and reassurance. We know that the criminal will be apprehended and order, at least to some extent, restored. Present-tense narration takes away that sense of security and comfort.

By placing the reader in the narrative present, the author denies them the consolation of the already-happened, and in so doing also removes the authority of the investigator. If we follow the investigator in the present, as her story unfolds, we are less certain of the outcome. In addition, the third-person removes Scarpetta's authority. Where once she was in charge of her own story, she is now the observed. The theme of surveillance is a recurrent one in the Scarpetta series, and the use of third-person narrative underscores its relevance to the investigator's own fortunes. Most novels in the series feature a climactic scene during which Scarpetta is threatened by the forces she is trying to combat, but as long as she is the narrator her immunity is guaranteed. Taking that guarantee away places the investigator closer to the role of the victim. The switch from first- to third-person narration can be seen to mirror changes in the reading public's attitudes to forensic science, or science in general. Just as it is hard to appreciate now how original and exciting Poe's use of the clue was in

---

[75] 'This novel [classic crime fiction] contains not one but two stories: the story of the crime and the story of the investigation', writes Todorov. In the hardboiled novel, though, '[w]e are no longer told about a crime anterior to the moment of the narrative'. T. Todorov, 'The Typology of detective fiction', in *The Poetics of Prose*, trans. Richard Howard (Cornell University Press, 1977) pp. 139–41.

'The Murder in the Rue Morgue', it is hard to remember a time when the extensive and sustained application of forensic science in the solving of crime was new. The proliferation of forensic crime narratives, coupled with a growing mistrust of science made possible by the rise of social media and the ease of spreading of misinformation, have altered attitudes to scientific expertise.

Professor Nic Daeid made an analogous observation when asked to reflect on the public's belief in the infallibility of science:

> Science at its absolute core is often something that is constantly evolving. And so our position is constantly shifting. As we measure more we're becoming either more certain about our position or less certain about our position. As scientists we are very comfortable with that, but other people are not, especially with the idea of less certainty. In court we are often asked to say, did this happen or not? And we may say, well, we don't know, or this is the evidence I have to support the occurrence but that does not absolutely say that the event happened. And so the trustworthiness of science is a really big issue.

Uncertainty is the enemy of the forensic crime novel. Solving crime and bringing criminals to justice depends upon the belief that the scientific expert's answers are definitive. Where the crime novel does leave some room for uncertainty is in its attitudes to criminality. Forensic science can measure, categorise, and explain, but human nature, especially in its extremes, remains a mystery. Section 3 examines the role and evolution of the criminal in the forensic crime novel, seeking to understand whether a different type of investigation (the forensically driven one) also requires a different type of criminal.

3 Catching Criminals

There is a strong correlation between forensic crime novels and novels featuring sensational murders and perpetrators capable of extreme acts of sadism and violence, as well as serial killers. The pursuit of such criminals requires the services of forensic psychiatrists, psychological profilers, and a host of other experts who attempt to contain and account for criminal behaviour. Despite the reading public's fascination with forensic science, and their belief in its infallibility, these books also hint at the limits of science, suggesting that it cannot fully explain evil or criminality. This section examines the cultural meaning of the killer in forensic crime fiction as well as their function within the genre. Whereas in earlier forms of crime fiction the criminal and the investigator are depicted as doubles, or at least in possession of overlapping characteristics, forensic crime fiction relies on a clearer demarcation of good and evil, which often occurs along gendered lines. What is the relationship between the acts of extreme sadism and violence depicted in these novels and the scientific rigour and discipline that goes into uncovering them? What attitudes to criminality do these novels typically exhibit, and how are they different from those seen in other types of crime fiction? Given that most brutal killers in forensic crime fiction are men, and most victims are women, this section also examines how we have moved from the doubling of the detective with the criminal (a predominantly male relationship) to an affinity between the forensic expert and the victim (predominantly female).

In its general attitude to criminality, the forensic crime novel, most closely though not exclusively associated with white authors and characters, resembles the wider genre within which it belongs: the white-authored police procedural. Crime novels written by people of colour are much more likely to focus on the social conditions of crime, and criminality is seen not as an aberration but as a direct consequence of inequality, poverty, racism, and other structural problems that beset the society in which the novel is set. This might also explain why there are fewer examples of forensic crime fiction written by people of colour: the belief in the power of institutions and the strength of material evidence sits uncomfortably with those who know that justice isn't always served in these terms. The emphasis of the forensic crime novel on the killer as an aberration rather than a product of social problems is continuous with the police procedural's similarly polarised view. Nevertheless, at their best, both the police procedural and the forensic crime novel do not only satisfy our desire for the restoration of order and justice through the triumph of good over evil. They also go further, to question the causes of criminality and to expose the limits of scientific enquiry. In addition, while some writers treat crime as a local problem specific to the community that their characters operate in, others opt to highlight a trans-border or global perspective. Cornwell and Reichs are good examples of the two ends of the spectrum. As Nicole Kenley argues, their depictions of criminality not only reveal contrasting attitudes to the containment of evil, they also link with wider questions about the epistemology of crime:

> Both globalisation and Postmodernism begin to impact American detective fiction around the same time as the contemporary forensic trend, yet they are often thought of as working at cross purposes. Yet while globalisation and Postmodernism each suggest that crimes simply may not be resolvable, the rise of forensic detective fiction points yet again to detective fiction's foundational drive toward containment.[76]

---

[76] N. Kenley, 'Teaching American detective fiction in the contemporary classroom', in C. Beyer (ed.), *Teaching Crime Fiction* (London: Palgrave Macmillan, 2018), p. 72.

It is true that the forensic novel as a genre challenges the postmodernist preoccupation with the dismantling of grand narratives and their replacement with little stories – stories whose proliferation is aided by globalisation. The belief in the infallibility of forensic science can be seen as restorative, legitimising science and emphasising the availability of empirically derived truths. Yet the depiction of criminals in the forensic crime novel suggests a counternarrative: either evil exists in ways that science cannot comprehend, or it exists in complex networks that forensic science cannot combat. Kenley sees Patricia Cornwell at one end of the spectrum, 'representing the idea that forensics offer a genuine strategy for effecting control of threats, and Kathy Reichs at the other end, expressing extreme doubt about the possibility of forensic science to genuinely contain or control crime'.[77]

The rapists and killers of women that dominate Cornwell's plots are depicted as evil individuals in the service of evil. This explains why Lee and Katharine Horsley think that a lot of the novels of this type should be studied through the lens of the gothic and its preoccupation with evil as a force of nature, and with the abject.[78] In *Body of Evidence*, Scarpetta muses that murder 'never emerges full blown from a vacuum. Nothing evil ever does.'[79] There is an attempt to give the novel's perpetrator a troubled family history and, much more controversially, a psychiatric disorder, but the unnecessary shooting of the killer once he has been incapacitated points to another narrative: one where Scarpetta, representing the forces of the law and of good and decent human behaviour, vanquishes and punishes the deranged 'other' whose murderous lust is not fully explained or excused by his troubled background. In addition, as Joy Palmer notes, Cornwell's novels are conservative and fail to challenge the status quo through their use of queer and socially deviant characters as personifications of evil.[80] Heidi Strengell also argues that 'Cornwell's monsters are created to evoke disgust and fear. Similarly, otherness – sexual, political, racial, and ethnical – is at stake in her work.'[81] Cornwell's killers are depicted as 'monsters' that exist in the margins of society, and they often suffer from physical medical conditions that mark them out as 'other'. Writing in the 1990s, when HIV contamination was a grave fear, and AIDS was more or less a death sentence, Cornwell introduced into her novels ideas and images around contagion that reflected and amplified fears that were circulating in the real world. Many of the novels end with a climactic scene in which Scarpetta is assaulted by

---

[77] Ibid.   [78] K. and L. Horlsey, 'Body language', 5.   [79] Cornwell, *Body of Evidence*, p. 312.
[80] Palmer, 'Tracing bodies', 71.
[81] H. Strengell, '"My knife is so nice and sharp I want to get to work right away if I get a chance": Identification between author and serial killer in Patricia Cornwell's Kay Scarpetta Series', *Studies in Popular Culture*, 27 (October 2004), 73–90 (90).

the criminal. The threat is both real and figurative; as well as her life being in danger, Scarpetta runs the metaphorical danger of being infected by the criminal. Her home is depicted as a safe space with advanced security features: a space where she can be protected from the evil she fights in the course of her job. Therefore, an invasion of the home by the criminal carries the connotation of contagion: evil comes into the safe home – the serpent, as Auden would have it, arriving in the Garden of Eden.[82]

Kathy Reichs approaches the question of evil in a different way: 'I don't want to do one serial killer theme after another. I'm looking at violence from different perspectives. In the first book, there was a serial killer; in the second, it was a cult; the third is bikers (violence for profit); the fourth is a plane crash; the fifth is human rights issues.'[83] Her modest account of the choice of killer would suggest that her contribution to the genre lies in diversity, but in reality she has achieved much more than that. Whereas the first couple of novels in the Temperance Brennan series suggest a preoccupation with evil quite similar to Cornwell's, as the series unfolds Reichs adds nuance and context. In *Death du Jour* (2000) the killer is a cult leader, a woman whose name is Elle. '*Je suis Elle*. I am she. The female force', Elle tells Brennan.[84] Whereas the figure of the female pathologist represents the 'female force' as the force of giving/restoring life, here Reichs explores its dark double. Cornwell has also created memorable female killers, but they exist as self-contained representations of evil. Reichs uses a sub-plot involving a nun in order to contrast Elle's murderous ambition with the nun's desire to serve and hep others. In addition, the story involves Brennan's sister joining the dangerous cult. The sister enters the cult through a legitimate route, taking a university course that leads her there. The contrast between the university course and the cult highlights the permeability of legitimate and illegitimate institutions, thereby figuratively blending the spheres of good and evil rather than keeping them separate.

In *Grave Secrets* (2002), the author uses her personal experience and expertise to focus on human rights violations in Guatemala, a move that takes her far from the trope of the serial killer with which she started her series. A later novel, *Bones of the Lost* (2013), takes on trafficking and American involvement in Afghanistan, thereby taking the crime novel away from the preoccupation with evil as a gothic trope, instead exploring its political and transnational dimensions. Lili Pâquet has examined the theme of travel in Reichs's work, arguing

---

[82] W. H. Auden, 'The Guilty Vicarage', p. 158.

[83] A. Dunn, 'PW talks with Kathy Reichs', *Writing Forensics: Publishers Weekly* (May 5, 2003). www.publishersweekly.com/pw/by-topic/authors/interviews/article/33858-writing-forensics.html.

[84] K. Reichs, *Death du Jour* (London: Arrow Books, 2000), p. 418.

that this transnational dimension also allows the author to highlight 'how different institutions and justice systems let down their female citizens.'[85] Evil in this case no longer applies to the aberrant individual, but to ideologies and institutions that allow violence against women to continue.

Tess Gerritsen's 'Rizzoli and Isles' series can be usefully compared to Cornwell's. Both rely heavily on sensationalised brutal murders of women, and both tend to depict evil as a force of nature. However, where Cornwell depicts Scarpetta as a lone crusader, a woman set apart by her scientific expertise and her status as a woman with no children, Gerritsen emphasises the importance of female solidarity. Like Scarpetta, Maura Isles feels vulnerable and at time helpless in the presence of evil. In *The Sinner*, for example, she fears that she is being watched and recalls 'the prey's cold sense of dread when it suddenly realizes it is being stalked'.[86] Her partnership with Rizzoli, however, provides security and protection that are very different from the kind that Marino has to offer to Scarpetta. Similarly, in *The Surgeon* Jane Rizzoli comes under attack in a way that turns her from investigator to victim. On the trail of the killer known as 'the Surgeon', Rizzoli attempts to save victim Catherine Cordell. She walks into a trap and is incapacitated by the Surgeon, only to be saved by Cordell herself. The reversal of victim and saviour provides a figurative showcase of the value of female solidarity that becomes more important in subsequent novels in the series, but the narrative does not end there. Unusually, *The Surgeon* gives the last word to the serial killer. The novel has a conventional ending that involves suspense, the main female investigator coming into danger, violence and action, followed by the apprehension and punishment of the criminal and the wedding of two of the novel's positive characters. Where most novels in the genre would have ended there, Gerritsen adds one final chapter to hers. It is narrated in italics by the killer, now safely held in a secure prison, away from other inmates because of his notoriety. The continuing obsession of the incarcerated killer accomplishes two things: on the level of generic convention, it hints that this murderer might come back: perhaps he will escape prison; perhaps he will find an accomplice to carry out his work for him. After all, this is how many novels that are part of a series work (spoiler alert: he does escape). On a different narrative level, giving the last word to the killer subverts the convention which demands the excision of evil and the return to a state of prelapsarian innocence. Gerritsen suggests that even if evil is contained, in the world of the prison, and also in the world of the police procedural, we cannot assume that it ceases to exist.

---

[85] L. Pâquet, 'Kathy Reichs's Contiki crime: Investigating global feminisms', *Clues* 33.1 (2015), 51–61 (p. 51).

[86] T. Gerritsen, *The Sinner* (London: Penguin, 2023), p. 222.

The fact that the serial killer's first-person narrative frames the novel points to a belief that evil exceeds human understanding and eludes rational explanation. Interviewed on the occasion of the publication of *The Mephisto Club*, Gerritsen was asked 'Do you believe that a place can be evil?' 'Sometimes you wonder whether there is a portal for bad things to come out', she replied. 'I also feel that there's a genetic or biological basis for why certain people commit terrible acts.'[87] Val McDermid, on the other hand, believes that criminality is largely determined by social factors such as deprivation and inequality:

> I don't believe in evil. Some people write about evil as if it were something you catch without a vest on but I don't think evil exists. I think it's a cop-out to say that it does. People do evil things, people do terrible things, but there are reasons for that. Most people I write about who commit terrible acts have terrible acts in their own background. These things happen out of circumstance, experiential circumstance; people's lives are damaged and that damage manifests itself sometime in acts of horror. But I don't think anyone is born evil. I think what we should be aiming for is to eradicate the awful things that often happen in childhood that shape people.

McDermid's views demonstrate that forensic science fiction is a capacious genre. It can successfully accommodate contrasting views of criminality whilst maintaining its commercial appeal. The reason for that could well be the application of forensic science in the solving of crime: as long as logic, reason and science prevail, the origins of criminality are of secondary interest to many readers.

Because of its emphasis on extreme sadism and serial killers who are far removed from society, the forensic novel does not lend itself to a doubling of the criminal and the investigator in the way that other sub-genres do. The Continental Op, Sam Spade, and Philip Marlowe share traits with gangsters, for example, while the character of the gentleman thief, or the 'good' serial killer embodied by Luther, provide a literalisation of this duality. At its best, the crime novel can suggest that there is but a thin line that separates illegal activity from the investigative actions that lead to the apprehension of criminals. This is one of the complex ways in which the crime novel can both support the status quo and interrogate it, shining a light on practices whose legality and legitimacy can be questionable. As Gill Plain notes, '[a]ny examination of the crime genre soon reveals the impossibility of maintaining a clear division between guilt and innocence, law and the criminal'. Plain suggests that there is a long tradition of 'amalgamation of hunter and killer', and argues that this amalgamation can

---

[87] S. Anable, 'I'm no angel: PW talks with Tess Gerritsen'. www.publishersweekly.com/pw/by-topic/authors/interviews/article/10352-i-m-no-angel.html.

point to two things: the critique of the forces of law and order, but also the idea that 'to catch a killer you must think like a killer'. Plain's main argument is that 'the boundary between detective and criminal, the law and its others, has become so permeable that the genre is collapsing'.[88] 'For writers such as William McIllvaney and George P. Pelecanos crime is fundamentally a product of social contamination', Plain argues, whereas for Ian Rankin and Val McDermid 'crime is predominantly social'. Hinting at a transatlantic divide, Plain goes on to suggest that for Patricia Cornwell, 'contamination is not the issue, and while crime might spread like a plague, moral immunity is granted to righteous Americas. In Cornwell's world serial killers are evil, pure and simple, and good virtuous pathologists exist to root them out'.[89] What Plain does not dwell upon is the fundamental difference between fictional police officers and forensic scientists. Whereas the former are often depicted as corrupt and complicit in the system that perpetuates evil wrongdoing, the latter are indeed depicted as saviours untouched by the corruption around them. Pete Marino is far from being the morally uncompromised and righteous American, but then he represents the police department. Scarpetta, on the other hand, is indeed a virtuous upholder of law, truth, and justice, and I suggest that it is her scientific knowledge and expertise that place her in that position. Forensic science is therefore seen as a corrective to corruption and contamination, and scientists become the new saviours of a genre at risk of collapse. This is less true of forensic fiction that uses a scientist as one of the main investigators. In the forensic crime novel, criminals and investigators are usually depicted as polar opposites, embodying ideas of the fight between good and evil with clearly demarcated lines. Many of these narratives promote a view of criminality that is incompatible with the values of the police and the forensic scientists. The scientists in these books are heroic saviours, while the criminals are monstrous and removed from mainstream society. The fact that science and technology can help win this battle between opposing forces is what gives the forensic crime novel its considerable consolatory power.

And yet, forensic crime novelists have found ways to tap into the cultural fascination with the criminal/investigator duality. In Deaver's *The Bone Collector*, for example, the perpetrator turns out to be the investigator's own physician. The idea that a person who has the power to heal is also the person who destroys life is also taken up by Simon Beckett. In the first book of his Dr David Hunter series, the killer is a doctor; not only that, Dr Hunter has been working closely with him because the killer is capable of keeping up a façade of

---

respectability. In a lot of forensic crime fiction, the killer remains hidden and elusive, but here he is hiding in plain sight, taking the novel closer to the tradition that Catherine Ross Nickerson discusses, where 'the identity of the killer may truly be a cipher in the real world, within the confines of the detective novel', but 'the perpetrator is known to us'.[90] In both cases, the killers use their medical training and scientific knowledge for evil purposes, thus providing a counterpoint to the idea of the benign scientist or physician. What is at stake in these cases is primarily a competition for the possession and application of knowledge. Lin Anderson also dramatises this competition; in *Sins of the Dead*, suspicions grow that a killer is attending a forensic science course at the University of Glasgow where Rhona McLeod and her colleagues teach investigative methods for crime-solving. Deaver, meanwhile, increasingly turns to digital crime. In so doing, he enables criminal and investigator to compete in a world where physical strength is no longer a requirement, but also a world where resourcefulness rather than an expensive and long education bestow knowledge. Digital crime democratises the forensic novel; whereas few criminals would have the resources to become experts in forensic science, many can access training and knowledge that enables them to commit and cover up crime in the digital sphere. This uncoupling of crime and investigation from the physical and material world has implications for the future of the forensic crime novel that, as yet, it may be too early to explore.

Deaver is notable not only for his interest in digital crime, but also for the use of a quadriplegic investigative protagonist. Whereas Patricia Cornwell uses illness and bodily dysfunction as amplifiers of criminal identities, Deaver proposes a literalisation of the idea that the investigator need not be a 'man of action'. For the purposes of plot expediency and generic appeal, Lincoln Rhyme has a crime-solving partner who is not disabled, but he remains the protagonist of the series. Rhyme embodies the idea of the investigator as an analytical thinker, but he also represents more than that. Rhyme was injured in the course of his work as a NYPD officer. A falling beam 'breaks' his body, while his creator breaks from the police procedural to introduce a liminal figure: an investigator who is and is not a police officer, a man who pursues criminals even though he cannot literally pursue anyone. By transferring illness and disability from the criminals and the victims to the detective, Deaver makes visible the genre's reliance on ableist tropes that equate physical imperfection either with villainy or with victimhood. His fiction works as a generic corrective, moving the representation of criminality or evil away from associations

---

[90] C. Ross Nickerson, 'Introduction: The satisfactions of murder', in Ross Nickerson (ed.), *The Cambridge Companion to American Crime Fiction* (Cambridge University Press, 2010), p. 1.

with illness. The series further shows that Rhyme's investigative powers are an adequate means of exerting control over the criminal world.

Nicole Kenley notes that, if Cornwell and Reichs represent two ends of the spectrum, Deaver 'offers a midpoint along this continuum':

> Jeffrey Deaver, particularly in his newer novels, focuses less on physical and more on digital evidence. His texts call attention to the dangers of computer technology and the misleading qualities of seemingly reliable data, while still maintaining faith in the ability of the detective (rather than merely the technology he or she wields). *The Broken Window* illustrates this simultaneous trust in and undermining of new digital technologies through its focus on data mining and the difficulties of containing digital crime, though again other Deaver novels could also achieve this purpose. In *The Broken Window*, Deaver's quadriplegic detective Lincoln Rhyme demonstrates the powers and the limits of digital technology, arguing that the success of these technologies remain contingent on the skilful detective.[91]

Despite the strength and popularity of the Lincoln Rhyme series, a suspicion remains that Deaver had to create a quadriplegic character because other types of investigator were becoming overused, rather than because he wished to make a point about ableism in crime fiction. Either way, his creation has contributed to the process of generic renovation that is necessary for all types of genre fiction, not only through the introduction of a differently abled protagonist, but also through the emphasis on the rise of digital crime and the need for digital forensic investigation.

What the future holds for forensic crime fiction remains to be seen. Val McDermid was asked to reflect on this, and she began by pointing out that forensic crime fiction is now so dominant that it is more or less synonymous with crime fiction:

> I don't think it is a sub-genre anymore. Increasingly it dominates the field because if you're writing contemporary crime fiction, even if it's cosy fiction, you can't ignore the realities of scientific investigation. Where the science goes, fiction has to follow, unless you want to write something set in the 1930s in a vicarage. The degree to which the science features will vary from writer to writer, but I think it's here to stay.

McDermid's view seems more optimistic than Plain's. Where Plain believes that the genre will collapse because the lines of demarcation between criminal and investigator get blurred, McDermid may be right to point out that fiction will continue to follow the science. Attitudes to science and scientists change, though, and relationships between scientists and police officers can be fraught

---

as often as they are fruitful. The figure of the forensic scientist has introduced a whole new element to the investigator/criminal binary, and even though in real life scientists are not involved in investigation and crime-solving to the extent that they are in fiction, their presence in the crime novel is reassuring: they suggest that the application of science has the power to restore order and contain evil. The consolation that science brings to the investigation of crime is likely to remain one of its key strengths, though, like Deaver, writers will continue to question the powers and limits of science and technology. In *Unnatural Causes*, Richard Shepherd looks back on his long career as a real-life forensic patholo-gist. He begins with the story of a rare mass shooting in the UK, and describes the atmosphere in the Westminster mortuary where secretary Pam Derby makes the necessary preparations:

> Pam was familiar with the emotional, unplanned chaos of real homicides. That's why she and the other staff, for relaxation, often read neatly plotted whodunits, where the murderer leaves clear clues and at the end the pieces of the jigsaw click into place. It's all so different from the many versions of the truth, the conflicting facts and interpretations of them which are the messy face of real investigations.[92]

Professor Nic Daeid said something similar when asked to reflect on compari-sons between the forensic scientist and the forensic crime novelist: 'I suppose the difference is that for our work we may never really get to the answer, because sometimes we end up with what we just don't know or we just can't tell.' Forensic science, it seems, is less consolatory in real life than it is in fiction, and while some authors will continue to treat science as the guarantor of truth, others will continue to reveal its inherent uncertainties. Nicole Kenley sees in forensic crime fiction a 'continuum of containment', with authors such as Cornwell reassuring readers of 'stability in the face of a rapidly changing global landscape', and others such as Reichs and Deaver demonstrating 'a far less stable state of affairs'.[93] The continued popularity of other sub-genres, such as domestic noir and cosy crime, make it harder to conclude whether crime fiction as a whole is popular because of its power to console or because of its potential to disturb and unsettle. That, in turn, makes it harder to predict which genre or sub-genre might gain ascendancy in a world where global security and environ-mental catastrophe are seen as major destabilising forces. In the ongoing process of generic renewal, the only certainty is that authors will continue to recalibrate the relationship between closure and uncertainty that gives the genre so much of its power.

---

[92] R. Shepherd, *Unnatural Causes* (London: Penguin, 2019), p. 13.
[93] N. Kenley, 'Global crime', p. 109.

Appendix 1
Interview with Professor Niamh Nic Daeid

Conducted at the University of Dundee, UK, on 23 June 2023

AV: You are the director of the Leverhulme Research Centre for Forensic Science at the University of Dundee. Tell me a little about the work undertaken at the centre.

NND: This centre is very different, probably in the UK or I would even go further and say around the world, from other research centres in forensic science. And it's different because the nature of the work that we do here is predominantly disruptive in a positive way. What we're interested in doing is looking at engagement with our whole community: from the crime scene examiners to the lawyers who oversee some of that examination, to the police officers who investigate crimes, to the scientists who use their skills and talents to look at evidence, and then to prosecutors, defenders, the judiciary, and the public. So, the whole spectrum. We engage all of these communities to talk about 'big ticket' issues. What is discussed is the art of the possible. What is it we want the future to look like? What does forensic science currently look like? And how do we get from one to the other?

AV: Can you tell me a little bit more about the relationship between the centre and the police?

NND: We probably work less with the police than we do with the legal and forensic science side because the police are very much involved in that first focus on the investigation. And so our work with the police is around the front end of what happens at the crime scene. Because, equally, what the police are mainly interested in is to use science as a tool, but they may not always be that focused on how science works. Neither, I would say, in some instances, are they that invested in the limitations of science. They just want it to work. And so that can occasionally lead to some tensions because, of course, the scientists may say 'this is the result I've got, but it has to be looked at in this context'. And sometimes that 'but' is missed out because the police have got a prosecutorial focus rather than the independent focus that the scientists have. So there may occasionally be some tension between the two. In the early stages of an investigation, one of the roles of the forensic scientist is to communicate really clearly to police officers with respect to what evidence types may possibly be at a scene depending on the alleged activity and also what evidence those items, those traces recovered, may possibly provide in terms of information about the events that unfolded at the scene in question. The work of the forensic scientist is also about managing the expectations of our colleagues simply to say even though they've seen this on the television, the science actually doesn't work like that, or it's more complicated, as well as managing expectations around different evidence types, as we're not always going to get a DNA profile from samples because actually DNA degrades over time or there is known prior contact between the parties involved in an allegation. The investigative space can be very fast flowing, so information is often needed quickly so that the police can move their investigation along as quickly as possible. The initial investigation phase is also almost always prosecutorially focused. Where we've had more interaction with the police is around digital evidence, because that, more often than not, remains within the realm of policing; that may be changing in Scotland, but in England and Wales, those who undertake digital evidence case work are mostly working within police forces.

AV: Critics claim that forensic evidence, in the way that it is represented in a novel, is often misleading because it seems to be a large part of the investigation, whereas in real life it tends to be used more as kind of supplementary evidence – for example, to secure a conviction. Are you saying that this does tend to be the case?

NND: Forensic evidence is often circumstantial evidence; it arises as a circumstance of the events that might have unfolded and it's rarely, if ever, the smoking gun – and that's an important concept that people who work within the space have an understanding of, whether those are police officers or lawyers or other investigators. Our job as scientists sometimes involves going to scenes. I would say that the use of science and the scientific approach begins at the scene, not in the laboratory, and that is rarely highlighted in fictional representations. We recover traces, and then what we do with them in scientific analysis is almost always corroborative. So it's not going to be necessarily the thing that points to one individual or another, with perhaps the exception of fingerprints. That said, in the 1980s, when we saw the advent of DNA technology, in the early days DNA was certainly used as a scientific technique that could point towards a person of interest or potential offender. Nowadays that's not so certain, and that is because our technology has become much more sensitive. However, that sensitivity doesn't come with increased selectivity, which means that the technology is more sensitive to identifying the presence of people's DNA; what you now commonly end up with, then, is a mixture of DNA from people who've been in association with one another or may have touched, or been in the vicinity of, an object, and so mixed DNA profiles are much more common. We've moved away from being able to look at a bodily fluid stain about the size of a fifty pence piece, which is what we needed in the 1980s to extract DNA and develop a single DNA profile, to where we can get DNA from a single cell, but we now get multiple mixed DNA profiles and we are challenged sometimes to say with certainty that DNA in a mixed sample comes from a particular individual. Fingermarks recovered from scenes can also be difficult to interpret if they do not contain sufficient detail.

We've got similar issues with non-biometric data. For example, how do we know that a fibre comes from a particular jumper? In order to understand that, we need to know how common the jumper is and how many jumpers of the same type may be associated within the environment of the crime scene. So, the forensic evidence is by no means providing us with a certainty, but it is used in the courts as a corroborative link. Lawyers describe the evidence presented in a court case like a chain, and the chain is only as strong as its weakest link. So if you have a weak link – whether it's an eyewitness testimony, or whether if's DNA evidence that isn't understood properly – that's where things start to break apart. For example, if we get multiple DNA profiles and our challenge is trying to sort them out, the person of interest's DNA might be in that mixture, but that does not necessarily imply that person is responsible for the alleged crime, only that their DNA might be present. In the way in which forensic scientists provide their evidence, we have a system which is called 'a hierarchy of propositions', which sets a level of possibilities at offence, activity, and source levels that may have generated the evidence type. So, if we are examining a fibre or a DNA profile, then we always evaluate the presence of that evidence based on more than one possibility or hypothesis or proposition. Often we deal with source-level propositions: does that DNA profile come from this individual? Or does that fibre come from this jumper? And we're not always able to answer that question because we don't know how many similar jumpers there may be, or the DNA profile may be difficult to interpret. That gives you a real positioning of what the forensic scientific evidence is there to do, which is not to be the smoking gun, but to be the corroboration of a set of potential activities while also pointing out how that evidence might occur given a different set of possibilities.

AV: I think that leads me to a couple of questions. One is that what you describe is obviously very complex and potentially difficult for a non-scientist to understand. So how do you ensure that the police and other relevant stakeholders understand that complexity at a level that makes sense to them?

NND: A lot of that is by training, by working together and talking together. In Scotland we're in a very different position than England and Wales in terms of how we work together as a justice community. In Scotland if a crime occurs, after the 999 call reporting it to the police, the police will then engage the procurator fiscal. The investigation will begin, and the procurator fiscal is the individual that works with the police to understand what investigation needs to be undertaken. So, in Scotland, the lawyers are involved from the very beginning, and they will be involved in discussing with the scientists what evidence needs to be examined; and before that evidence is even examined, there will often be a discussion about the limitations that might be involved. That's a really interesting model because it's one that, from the very start, requires collaboration and discussion and explanation by the scientists to the non-scientists. The question may be that if you want me to do DNA analysis I can do that, but in this case I'm not sure it will add value, and this is the reason why and these are the limitations. In England and Wales the police are in charge of the investigation. The lawyers only come into it further down the line; it's the police officers who will make decisions about what science they want involved. They will often speak with the scientists, but at the end of the day it's their call. So there may be much less collaborative discussion. And here you're relying on the police officers to know what they're talking about to some degree, which is a little difficult and possibly unfair on them because they're not scientists. There may be much less discussion, and the discussion may often be about money and how much different tests will cost. How much will it cost me to do a DNA profile, for example? In England and Wales, the forensic science services are commercial, the service supplied is monetised. The police who need the evidence analysed pick from a menu that tells them how much it's going to cost get different tests done. And so the people making the decisions about 'should we do this piece of science or not?' are often non-scientists watching budgets. And that's a very uncomfortable position for scientists to be in, because when the case is presented in court, there's an expectation that there will be scientific evidence if that's the nature of the case, and if it hasn't been undertaken it's not the scientists' fault. The people making the decisions are the police officers or the prosecution service, but often in the absence of the scientists; the scientists just get told what to do. And so it's a really different model in terms of who makes the decisions. The science is often quite straightforward – the data, analysis of samples – however, what the results mean in context is the bit that's more complicated and that's where the scientists are guided by what we call the hierarchy of propositions.

AV: And I think it's definitely last in fictional accounts of it.

NND: I think it isn't and it isn't. There are some crime writers that work really hard to do their research with forensic scientists and with pathologists and police officers, and try to get as broad an understanding as they can of how the whole thing works. And their books are the richer for it, I think. Some of them work pretty hard to try to understand all of these different elements, but also the limitations of the science used.

AV: Do you have an example that you could tell me a little bit more about, of an author who does those things?

NND: There's a couple. We do a reasonable amount of work with Val McDermid. She does quite a lot of hard work to get the science background right, and so she'll come and she'll speak with us around ideas she wants for a book or a particular pieces of science she wants to involve and we'll go through it. There are also some forensic scientists who are also crime writers. Kathy Reichs is a great example: she's a forensic anthropologist and the quality of the scientific discussion in her books is really high. I remember reading one of her books and she is describing a fire scene in it; her description was really good and accurate in terms of what you were looking at and what inference you could draw from what you were looking at. And others like Ian Rankin are really good as well with regard to background research. His books often include more around police procedures.

AV: It's good to know that not too much of it is made up, entirely fictional. But I think one thing that is always different in books is the extent to which the scientist is involved with the investigation; I think sometimes they're depicted as doing it out of personal interest, to help bring justice to the victims and the families and so on. So how removed from reality is that idea?

NND: That's very far from reality. As scientists, forensic scientists, we're impartial and work for the Courts. Forensic scientists cannot get emotionally involved in cases, and mostly we don't get involved with speaking to witnesses or anything else, with one or two notable exceptions. We are very conscious of bias. Whereas on television you'll see the forensic pathologists and others working or interacting directly with victims or relatives of victims. That doesn't happen in the real world.

AV: What fascinates me, then, is this idea that in the novel it is as you described: there is the emotional involvement and there is a level of subjectivity that, as you point out, would not exist in the real world. And yet the science itself is still seen as totally objective and neutral. So I think maybe the novel tries to reconcile those two.

NND: Yes, that that's good point, I mean possibly, when you look at forensic science, the different elements of it, some of the work that we do absolutely involves objective questions. So if we're analysing a drug, for example, then you extract the drug from the powder, pill, or potion and you dissolve it in a solvent and you inject it into a machine and the machine will then analyse it chemically and then you can look it up in a library or compare it to a standard and identify the compounds present in the sample. So it's a very straightforward, objective scientific technique. Other areas of forensic evidence are not objective. They are almost entirely subjective, such as the comparison of fingerprints and the linkage of bullets to guns. The comparison of tool marks, handwriting, footwear marks – all of those are almost wholly subjective analysis.

AV: That is really surprising to hear. I think many people will find that surprising to hear.

NND: When you're examining fingerprints you look at three different levels in the pattern that you can then compare. When a fingerprint examiner is looking at a mark that's recovered from a scene, so from an unknown source, it can often be incomplete. They can be messy, or may be smudged. And looking for a match is a pattern comparison task, which is a bit like spot the difference. There is no science involved. And it's the same with bullet comparison. When a bullet comes out of the barrel gun the gun barrel leaves little scrapes along the bullet which are called striation marks that are claimed to be unique to a gun. But this assertion has never been tested. When you're looking at two bullets that may have been fired from the same gun, then you're looking at these striation marks. You examine the bullet using a microscope and try to line up the striation marks on a test bullet fired from the suspected gun and a bullet from the scene. If there are more similarities than there are differences, then a conclusion may be made that the bullet could have come from the gun. This isn't science. Popular fiction treats all forensic science evidence as the same, because it's all treated as if it were science, but it isn't. Feature comparison doesn't always involve science. Whereas analysing drugs, DNA, ignitable liquids, explosives, and toxicology is robustly scientific. And it's something that I think is really interesting in the way that science is depicted in the courtroom and also in fiction. Because, as you said, everything is assumed to be science. And actually some of it isn't science at all.

AV: What we've seen during and after Covid is that there is so much misinformation, and it's also so very difficult for scientists to communicate complex scientific ideas. So, I have two questions for you. One: what are your thoughts on the extent to which the public, in a general way, trust or do not trust scientists? And my second question is: how challenging is it for you as a scientist to communicate science to a non-specialist audience?

NND: I think you're absolutely right to pick up the pandemic as a crucial point. The use of science occurred so fast in this country, in the UK, and we were constantly being told to follow the science and that the policy makers would follow the science. And, as a scientist, I was listening to this thinking you're going to make science the fall guy when things go wrong because you're going to say we're following the science as an absolute solution without actually understanding what you're talking about in terms of what science is, because science is inherently about measuring things, understanding the uncertainties and error rates associated with these measurements, and then coming up with theories and propositions based on data as to what might be going on. So it's slow. And it's meticulous. And it's evolutionary. It evolves over time as we start to understand more. So, when you follow the science to make a policy decision, then you're actually only following what you've done up to that point, and you're taking a risk in making that policy decision because science will continue forever and you learn more the more you measure things and generate data. Science at its absolute core is often something that is constantly evolving. And so our position is constantly shifting. As we measure more we're becoming either more certain about our position or less certain about our position. As scientists we are very comfortable with that, but other people are not, especially with the idea of less certainty. In court we are often asked to say, did this happen or not? And we may say, well, we don't know, or this is the evidence I have to support the occurrence but that does not absolutely say that the event happened. And so the trustworthiness of science is a really big issue. Most people out in the world trust scientists because of the nature and character of what we do and how we present our data and its limitations. It has an overall trustworthiness associated with it.

AV: The world of forensic investigation is dominated by women. So, first of all, in your experience, is that also true of the real world? And, also, do you have any theories as to why?

NND: That's a really, really good question. In the real world, there are a lot more women in the profession now than there were, say, thirty years ago. And women are achieving positions that are higher up the organisational tree. The rank-and-file of forensic science are women, and certainly when you look at universities that teach forensic science at Master's level, the student body is predominantly female, so women are attracted to this, but they don't always make it to the top. I don't know whether what's happening in crime novels is a sort of a rebellion against the face of reality, or an aspiration towards how it should be. I don't know. But if you look at novels like those of Lynda LaPlante, or Val McDermid, or Kathy Reichs, there are strong female characters at the top. In real life in the UK there are some professions, such as forensic anthropology, where actually most of the more senior practitioners are women.

AV: Why might that be?

NND: I don't know. It might because female scientists are very meticulous, so we're really attracted to the attention to detail. Forensic science is very meticulous, very much focused around attention to detail. I don't think it's to do with empathy because it's not that we don't have empathy, but that we have to cut it off to do our jobs properly. So you have to be able to just put your emotional connection with a case aside and be impartial.

AV: Before we conclude, I have to ask you, do you watch shows like *CSI*, or do they drive you crazy?

NND: I do watch them from time to time. Full disclosure, we worked with Val McDermid, and she convinced us to advise on a TV show which was called *Traces*. There's been two series of it, it's based in Dundee, and it's loosely based on our work. We were the scientific advisers to that series and we said we would only do it if they depicted the science accurately. Which they mostly did, to be fair. And so the science became almost a character in the story. So it wasn't, you know, you look at a sample, next thing look at a machine, and two seconds later you have a result. And the result says, yes, it absolutely is him, he did it. We said no, we can't do things like that and that was the only reason we got involved in it. I don't watch *CSI*. It's not something that I'm particularly interested in. I do watch some of the others from time to time. A lot of it is about providing entertainment for forty-five minutes, and they are very good at doing that. They really are. And so they take liberties with the scientific depiction. Of course they do. Because science is slow. It takes a lot longer than forty-five minutes to get answers out of the machines. So, they are what they are. But in terms of the picture of science in the real world, no. And it's also the characterisation of the scientists: as you said already, they get involved, they get sucked into the emotional story. And that doesn't happen in the real world because we would compromise ourselves in terms of being able to look at things in an unbiased way, as both the victims of crime and the people that are accused of crime have an expectation that we wouldn't.

AV: Can you reflect upon the similarities between what you do and what a crime novelist does?

NND: That's a really good question. Novelists and forensic scientists are both trying to communicate and often the communication's role is looking at an event that's a finite event: in other words, something happened. We need to use different tools that we might have in our toolbox to work out what happened. And then we need to convince people to make a decision about this. Or did something else happen? And the crime novel is the same. The weaving of it has red herrings scattered about the story to make you think you know who did it. And really good crime novels don't reveal that until the end. That's the gripping part of the story. And it's similar in real life, because we don't know the answer to the question before we start a story, but we're still trying to use our talents and our scientific expertise and our experiential knowledge to try to tease out what finding a particular thing actually means in the context of this case. And where are the gaps, where are the bits of the puzzle that are missing? That way, I suppose, our minds are working in a similar way. And so that there's that sort of puzzle-solving that that forensic scientists have to do. And it differs depending on the nature of the crime. If you're looking at a fire scene or at the scene of an explosion, where there may be lots of blood patterns, then a lot of that puzzle-solving is at the crime scene because you're looking at the puzzle in front of you. You're looking at the marks on the walls or how different furniture is burned in slightly different ways and you're using those physical clues in three dimensions to try to work out what the story of this fire is, what the narrative of that event has been. And so it's using lots of imagery to try to determine or understand the story. And novels are a bit like that as well. So I suppose the difference is that, in our work, we may never really get to the answer, because sometimes we just don't know or we just can't tell.

Appendix 2
Interview with Val McDermid

Conducted in Edinburgh, Scotland, on 17 August 2023

AV: I wanted to begin with the idea that, as critics have pointed out, there was a 'forensic turn' in crime fiction that took place some time in the mid-1990s. You started writing crime stories in the 1980s, so are you aware of a forensic turn in your own writing? Was there a time when you became more interested in forensic science?

VMcD: I have always been interested in forensic science. DNA was used in court for the first time in 1986 and because I was working as a journalist then, I was very much aware of it, and as a fledgling writer I wondered what that would mean for the crime novel. So right from the start I have been forensically aware. In my second novel I used, very tangentially, forensic computing analysis as it was in those days very, very basic, but I've been interested in how the science of forensic detection developed, so for me it's always been there in the background in my own work and I feel that my career has gone in lockstep with the development of forensics.

AV: And how do you research your science?

VMcD: I talk to people. Sometimes it's triggered by something that's in the press and then I will talk to people who know about it because I find that, not being a scientist myself, something is reported and I don't quite grasp it but talking to an expert, it becomes clear. And in my experience the forensic scientists I work with explain things very clearly; they are good and generous communicators, and you go to them with one question and you come back with three other things. So every time I talk to Niamh Nic Daeid or Sue Black or Lorna Dawson, I come back with new ideas in my head about something else too, so that has been for me a great spur to creativity.

AV: And does the science drive the plot, or do you already know who killed whom and why, and then the science comes in?

VMcD: Both. Sometimes I go to talk to someone about something that I know will be in that book, but then during the course of the conversation something else can come up. I remember one time talking to Sue Black about something completely different, and she started telling me about how your lymph nodes take ink from tattoos, so if you find a limbless torso you can tell from the lymph nodes that the victim had tattoos, and that gave me the idea for a novella called *Cleanskin*. I've been very lucky. I met Sue in the early 1990s and she became a keystone for a lot of my work, and Niamh too later on.

AV: Of course, and they've also been fictionalised in some of your work. You can learn so much from speaking to forensic scientists, but how much science is too much in a crime novel?

VMcD: I think you have to be careful not to fall in love with the technology. It's very seductive, but you put in what you have to put in. I try to avoid too detailed explanations because that's dull; it's about writing enough to convey the 'wow' factor, but not necessarily having to put in all the details of the science. And sometimes you read a novel where the author does not follow this advice and your eyes glaze over. That's not what you're trying to do with a crime novel. I see my function as to entertain but also to provoke thought and tell the reader things they didn't know, so I try to do it in a way that comes together as a whole, and not say 'here is a forensic science textbook.' It's also about bringing your life as a reader to your life as a writer, and asking, would I carry on reading if I read this?

AV: I also remember you saying once that if a crime novel was like real-life policing and investigations, it would be too dull and no one would read it. Do you think that applies to the application of forensic science as well?

VMcD: Yes, but in a funny way if you get the science right, the reader believes the rest of it. It is the investigative process that is in reality very tedious, but if you underpin your writing with details that readers recognise, and that can be forensic detail, or it could be a detail such as describing a street in a city or an atmosphere in a part of the city, so it's about anchoring in authenticity while telling lies [laughs].

AV: This something I'm trying to explore in my study: this balance between authenticity, believability, and being true to the science while also creating a coherent fictional world. Would you go as far as inventing some kind of forensic evidence, or do you absolutely believe that it has to be anchored in real science?

VMcD: You don't need to invent anything because there is so much that is real already. I am always amazed when I'm doing research into some aspect of forensic detail and I'm always on the alert for new developments.

AV: And also forensic science is moving very fast these days. So, are you aware of that problem: that a book may date quickly because of changes and developments in the science?

VMcD: Yes, but if you write a book that is set in real time then that is something that's going to happen so you have to not make it the keystone of what you're writing. When you talk to scientists, they'll tell you what's coming down the road so by the time your book comes out that has become a reality, so sometimes I find myself writing about something that isn't quite there yet but I've been told categorically that it is coming.

AV: You know a lot about forensic science because you've written a non-fiction book about it. As a novelist, you are obviously well equipped to communicate in a captivating manner, but you said earlier that you know scientists who are great communicators too. Good storytelling is at the heart of good science communication, but what comes with that is subjectivity, as well. So, when it comes to communicating science through stories, do you think the science becomes less reliable, less credible, can people question it more when it is in a story?

VMcD: I don't know. I think a lot of responsibility rests with the person who is narrating it. But I think most writers are keen to get things accurate and they value accuracy. The last thing you want is your inbox filling up with people telling you got it completely wrong.

AV: But also what became apparent during Covid was that there is a deep mistrust of science. Yet in forensic crime fiction there is a lot less of that. Everyone trusts forensic science. So do you think that forensic science occupies a special place, that everyone believes it even if they're less keen on other types of science?

VMcD: That's an interesting question, I hadn't considered that in those terms. You might be right, though. I suppose the tradition of the crime novel is that at the end there is a solution, at the end of it everything works out and order is restored, mostly, even though things don't necessarily go back to where they were in the beginning. But there is that sense that this is a form of storytelling that avoids chaos, that gives a positive outcome. We trust what we read in the crime novel because of the form of the novel, because of the shape of the story. But the same readers don't necessarily trust what the government or what scientists tell them.

AV: Do you think that's one of the reasons why the crime novel is so popular?

VMcD: It's comforting, there's a sense of comfort within the process. I did a book on female PIs a few years ago, and one of the real-life PIs told me that there is no closure; once you hand over the results of your investigation to your client that's it, you don't know what happens after that. She told me that she has helped lots of adopted people find their birth families, and when she has been there to witness the reunion it is like lightning striking someone else's house, and that idea stayed with me because that also works with the crime novel; it's comforting: they're getting murdered, I'm not getting murdered.

AV: I understand what you mean about the immense comfort that the reader can derive from reading crime novels, but at the same time you do not shy away from depictions of violence. And the violence in your books is grounded in the real: it is often sexual violence, or violence that takes place against a richly detailed historical background. So, more generally, how do you see the relationship between the reality of violence and the types of violence depicted in the crime novel?

VMcD: I've always thought that the crime novel should not be bloodless. There is a place for the cosy novel where you don't see bad things happening but, particularly when I'm writing the Tony Hill and Carol Jordan novels, when I'm writing about violence, I have to show what violence is and what it does and how it contaminates the lives of anyone who comes into contact with it. You have to tell people what's going on in order for them to understand the wider story you're telling them. It's a tightrope; it's a very careful line between what is enough and what is too much and that is something I'm very conscious of when I'm writing. And I hope that I have mostly got it right. I've said before that if you read these books and you're not disturbed, you probably need professional help. And I think women write about violence better than men because we've been taught that the world is a dangerous place. Men mostly write about violence from the outside, they describe what it is rather than how it feels.

AV: There was also a controversy a few years ago about the Staunch prize for a crime novel that did not depict violence against women.

VMcD: I thought that was absolutely absurd. You write about murder, you write about violence. I said at the time, when men stop committing terrible crimes of violence against women, I'm going to stop writing about them. I find it quite offensive to suggest that you can make the world a better place by not talking about reality.

AV: Now tell me a little bit more about female investigators. You started writing about female investigators in the 1980s, and they have remained central in your work.

VMcD: I'd been thinking about writing a crime novel for a while, but I couldn't figure out how to make it work because in the early 1980s in the UK all the crime novels were police procedurals or cosies and, as much as I loved them, I didn't want to write that kind of book. And then a friend of mine from university who had moved to America sent me a copy of Sara Paretsky's novel *Indemnity Only*. I found that really exciting; here was a character with a brain and a sense of humour, and, most of all, agency. She did her own heavy lifting; she didn't run to a guy for help when things got awkward. And what I also loved was the sense of politics. The story happened because of the struggles in people's lives, because of the work that they do; the novel had politics both on the big and also on the small scale of feminist politics. It really spoke to me, so I started reading other American feminist writers like Marsha Muller, Barbara Wilson, and Sue Grafton, and I thought this is the kind of thing I want to write. The one thing that I didn't find attractive as a writer was that they very much adopted the male model of the private eye, the loner, the maverick, and that didn't chime with my experience of female friendship. I felt that these women were not living the lives of what I understood to be modern feminists, and so Lindsay Gordon has friends, Kate Brannigan has friends, she has a network, and that's what I always had in mind. Carol Jordan doesn't really have friends, but that's because she's a different kind of person, but for me it's always been important to show female friendship as well as to write the crime story.

AV: Yes, and so much crime fiction of the time also reinforced a model of heteronormativity that obscured other types of relationships, networks, and solidarity.

VMcD: Yes, I did try not to fall for the heteronormativity model because that's not my life or the life of many women I know, even heterosexual ones.

AV: But how does that tie in with the idea that the crime novel as a genre is seen as fairly conservative in its politics, because law and order win the day and everything is restored at the end?

VMcD: I don't think that's necessarily the case. If you look at the politics of the crime novel now, they question social order and disrupt the social order. There may be some kind of restoration of order, there has to be some kind of resolution, but it's not necessarily about restoring the wider social picture.

AV: But to take this back to forensic science, could it be that this is a kind of compromise, that the crime novel will show that the world is imperfect and that order is not fully restored because there is no longer a belief in the concept, but there is that little pocket in the forensic science world where everything makes sense?

VMcD: That would be the case if forensic science was actually like that. So much of the science is also 'junk science', and Sue Black and Niamh Nic Daeid are working to debunk those myths about the infallibility of forensic science. So we have to be very careful about ascribing absolutism to the science. Sometimes the science is not science.

AV: And I think that's perhaps a discrepancy between forensic science in real life and forensic science as depicted in the crime novel, though clearly not in your fiction.

VMcD: I try to talk to people who practise; Dundee University has produced a series of primers about how to understand the science in the courtroom, and I think that's really important because forensic evidence is not always accurate. And even when the science is accurate, the interpretation of science isn't always.

AV: Let's move on to talk about villainy. How do you approach the idea of evil, who are your killers, and how do you imagine them? Are they completely evil, or are they multi-faceted human beings?

VMcD: I don't believe in evil. Some people write about evil as if it were something you catch without a vest on but I don't think evil exists. I think it's a cop-out to say that it does. People do evil things, people do terrible things, but there are reasons for that. Most people I write about who commit terrible acts have terrible acts in their own background. These things happen out of circumstance, experiential circumstance; people's lives are damaged and that damage manifests itself sometime in acts of horror. But I don't think anyone is born evil. I think what we should be aiming for is to eradicate the awful things that often happen in childhood that shape people.

AV: But do you think that crime fiction to some extent invites us to *not* think about the social causes of criminality? Not your fiction, obviously, but many of the novels out there depict evil as a force of nature, almost.

VMcD: That's just bad writing, and you get that anywhere, not just in crime novels. It's about not thinking things through properly.

AV: Traditionally the crime novel ends with the apprehension of the criminal, but we don't get to hear much about the aftermath of crime and punishment. Do you think crime fiction will move beyond that final curtain?

VMcD: I think it does already. It may not be the ones that are the number one in the bestseller lists, but those books are there. For example, Edinburgh writer Claire Askew's books feature a female cop whose brother ends up in prison, and the narrative explores the ongoing relationship between them and talks about the impact on them. So it's not just that vacuum of a bad man doing bad things. You just need to find a form to write that and shape it into a narrative.

AV: So what we're seeing is an evolution of the genre.

VMcD: I think the best thing about crime fiction is that there are no rules. When I started in the early 1980s it was a narrow genre, but since then it has exploded. The crime genre has a huge readership, so you can bend the form of the crime novel to tell any kind of story you like, and it's a subversive genre in those ways. If you want to write about subversive issues, you can dress them up in the form of the crime novel. It's a way to provoke thought. Not everyone does that, of course, but I like to write different kinds of crime novel.

AV: You are unusual in having so many successful series with different main characters and different kinds of investigation. Can you tell me a little bit about how or why you make these choices?

VMcD: After writing two Kate Brannigan novels, I wanted to do something different and challenge myself creatively. I discovered that I couldn't write two books back to back with the same character because I just got bored. Also, the Tony Hill and Carol Jordan novel was meant to be stand-alone, but when I finished writing it I realised that I was interested in the characters and their professions and wanted to write more.

AV: We as readers become attached to the characters. But do you think that this attachment to the investigator alters our view of the criminal or of the victim? Do we therefore have less sympathy for the other characters because so much of our emotional energy goes into our relationship with the investigators?

VMcD: I don't know. When I mentioned to some readers that Tony Hill and Carol Jordan might be coming back they got very excited, but they got even more excited when I mentioned that Jacko Vance might be coming back too, so I think they care about the villains and they care about the subsidiary characters as well.

AV: How do you compare the experience of writing about gruesome violence and having it depicted on TV?

VMcD: I don't like blood. I'm the one who looks away when someone gets stabbed in the eye.

AV: But how do you write about those things, then?

VMcD: I'm in control when I write, I'm constructing it, I know it's not real. When you watch something on TV it feels very real.

AV: What are your thoughts on the future of forensic crime fiction?

VMcD: I don't think it is a sub-genre anymore. Increasingly it dominates the field because if you're writing contemporary crime fiction, even if it's cosy fiction, you can't ignore the realities of scientific investigation. Where the science goes, fiction has to follow, unless you want to write something set in the 1930s in a vicarage. The degree to which the science features will vary from writer to writer, but I think it's here to stay.

Also, we need to consider that in the real world forensic science is not always used to solve crime. In England, forensic evidence is sent to private laboratories, and samples can be divided and sent to different labs until they become unusable. And there have been many cases where the forensic evidence has been called into doubt in the Court of Appeal because things were done on the cheap. There are also reports of jurors asking for DNA evidence when there are fingerprint and CCTV that provide sufficient proof. People can become blinded by science, too.

Select Bibliography

Anable, S. 'I'm no angel: PW talks with Tess Gerritsen', *Publishers Weekly* (August 4, 2006). www.publishersweekly.com/pw/by-topic/authors/interviews/article/10352-i-m-no-angel.html.

Auden, W. H. 'The guilty vicarage', in *The Dyer's Hand and Other Essays* (London: Faber and Faber, 1975), pp. 146–58.

Bell, S. *Crime and Circumstance: Investigating the History of Forensic Science* (Westport, CT: Praeger, 2008).

Belling, C. 'Reading the operation: Television, realism, and the possession of medical knowledge', *Literature and Medicine*, 17.1 (1998), 1–23.

Bergman, K. 'Fictional death and scientific truth: The truth-value of science in contemporary forensic crime fiction', *Clues: A Journal of Detection*, 30.1 (Spring 2012), 88–98.

Chou, J. 'Seeing bones speaking: The female gaze and the posthuman embodiment in Reichs's forensic crime fiction', *Concentric: Literary and Cultural Studies*, 38.1 (March 2012), 145–69.

Close, G. S. *Female Corpses in Crime Fiction: A Transatlantic Perspective* (London: Palgrave, 2018).

Cornwell, P. *Body of Evidence* (London: Warner, 1991).

Cornwell, P. *Point of Origin* (London: Warner, 1998).

Cornwell, P. *Postmortem* (London: Warner, 1990).

Dunn, A. 'PW talks with Kathy Reichs', *Writing Forensics: Publishers Weekly* (May 5, 2003).www.publishersweekly.com/pw/by-topic/authors/interviews/article/33858-writing-forensics.html

Foster, N. 'Strong poison: Chemistry in the works of Dorothy L. Sayers', in S. M. Gerber (ed.), *Chemistry and Crime: From Sherlock Holmes to Today's Courtroom* (Washington, DC: American Chemical Society, 1983), pp. 17–29.

Gerritsen, T. *The Sinner* (London: Penguin, 2023).

Gerritsen, T. *The Surgeon* (London: Ballantine Books, 2001).

Goulet, A. 'Crime fiction and modern science', in J. Allan, J. Gulddal, S. King, and A. Pepper (eds.), *The Routledge Companion to Crime Fiction* (London: Routledge, 2020), pp. 291–300.

Horsley, K. and L. 'Body language: Reading the corpse in forensic crime fiction', *Paradoxa*, 20 (2006), 1–30.

Howell, K. 'The suspicious figure of the female forensic pathologist investigator in crime fiction', *M/C Journal*, 15.1 (2012). https://doi.org/10.5204/mcj.454.

Jermyn, D. 'Labs and slabs: Television crime drama and the quest for forensic realism', *Studies in History and Philosophy of Biological and Biomedical Sciences*, 44 (2013), 103–9.

Kenley, N. 'Global crime, forensic detective fiction, and the continuum of containment', *Canadian Review of Comparative Literature*, 46 (2019), 96–114.

Kenley, N. 'Teaching American detective fiction in the contemporary classroom', in C. Beyer (ed.), *Teaching Crime Fiction* (London: Palgrave Macmillan, 2018), pp. 63–81.

Kennedy, J. G. 'The limits of reason: Poe's deluded detectives', *American Literature*, 47.2 (1975), 184–96.

Kirby, D. A. 'Forensic fictions: Science, television production, and modern storytelling', *Studies in History and Philosophy of Biological and Biomedical Sciences*, 44 (2013), 92–102.

Knight, S. *Form and Ideology in Crime Fiction* (Bloomington: Indiana University Press, 1980).

Kobialka, M. 'Delirium of the flesh: "All the dead voices" in the space of the now', in M. Bleeker (ed.), *Anatomy Live: Performance and the Operating Theatre* (Amsterdam: Amsterdam University Press, 2008) pp. 223–44.

Kristeva, J. *The Powers of Horror: An Essay on Abjection*, trans. L. S. Roudiez (New York: Columbia University Press, 1984).

Lucas, R. 'Anxiety and its antidotes: Patricia Cornwell and the forensic body', *Literature Interpretation Theory*, 15.2 (2010), 207–22.

Murley, J. *The Rise of True Crime: 20th-Century Murder and American Popular Culture* (Westport, CT: Praeger, 2008).

Palmer, J. 'Tracing bodies: Gender, genre, and forensic detective fiction', *South Central Review*, 18.3/4 (Autumn–Winter 2001), 54–71.

Pâquet, L. 'Kathy Reichs's Contiki crime: Investigating global feminisms', *Clues* 33.1 (2015), 51–61.

Pepper, A. *Unwilling Executioner: Crime Fiction and the State* (Oxford: Oxford University Press, 2016).

Plain, G. 'From "the purest literature we have" to "a spirit grown corrupt": Embracing corruption in twentieth-century crime fiction', *Critical Survey*, 20.1 (2008), 3–16.

Plain, G. *Twentieth-Century Crime Fiction: Gender, Sexuality and the Body* (Edinburgh: Edinburgh University Press, 2001).

Poe, E. A. *The Complete Tales and Poems of Edgar Allan Poe* (London: Penguin, 1982).

Poe, E. A. 'The philosophy of composition'. The Project Gutenberg eBook of The Raven and The Philosophy of Composition (no date). www.gutenberg .org/cache/epub/55749/pg55749-images.html.

Reichs, K. *Death du Jour* (London: Arrow Books, 2000).

Reichs, K. *Déjà Dead* (London: Arrow Books, 1997).

Ross Nickerson, C. 'Introduction: The satisfactions of murder', in C. Ross Nickerson (ed.), *The Cambridge Companion to American Crime Fiction* (Cambridge: Cambridge University Press, 2010), pp. 1–4.

Sawday, J. *The Body Emblazoned: Dissection and the Human Body in Renaissance Culture* (London: Routledge, 1995).

Shepherd, R. *Unnatural Causes* (London: Penguin, 2019).

Steenberg, L. *Forensic Science in Contemporary American Popular Culture: Gender, Crime, and Science* (London: Routledge, 2013).

Strengell, H. '"My knife is so nice and sharp I want to get to work right away if I get a chance": Identification between author and serial killer in Patricia Cornwell's Kay Scarpetta Series', *Studies in Popular Culture*, 27 (October 2004), 73–90.

Thomas, R. R. *Detective Fiction and the Rise of Forensic Science* (Cambridge: Cambridge University Press, 1999).

Todorov, T. *The Poetics of Prose*, trans. Richard Howard (London: Cornell University Press, 1977).

Vanacker, S. 'V. I. Warshawski, Kinsey Millhone and Kay Scarpetta : Creating a feminist detective hero', in P. B. Messent (ed.), *Criminal Proceedings: The Contemporary American Crime Novel* (London: Pluto Press, 1997), p. 62–77.

Wahrig, B. '"Nature is lopsided": Muscarine as scientific and literary fascinosum in Dorothy L. Sayers' *The Documents in the Case*', in H. Klippel, B. Wahrig, & A. Zechner (eds.), *Poison and Poisoning in Science, Fiction and Cinema*, Palgrave Studies in Science and Popular Culture (Cham: Palgrave Macmillan, 2017), pp. 57–73.

Whitman, W. 'When I heard the learn'd astronomer', The Walt Whitman Archive (no date). www.poetryfoundation.org/poems/45479/when-i-heard-the-learnd-astronomer.

Cambridge Elements ≡

Crime Narratives

Margot Douaihy
Emerson College

Margot Douaihy, PhD, is an assistant professor at Emerson College in Boston. She is the author of *Scorched Grace* (Gillian Flynn Books/Zando, 2023), which was named one of the best crime novels of 2023 by *The New York Times*, *The Guardian*, and *CrimeReads*. Her recent scholarship includes 'Beat the Clock: Queer Temporality and Disrupting Chrononormativity in Crime Fiction', a NeMLA 2024 paper.

Catherine Nickerson
Emory College of Arts and Sciences

Catherine Ross Nickerson is the author of *The Web of Iniquity: Early Detective Fiction by American Women* (Duke University Press, 1999), which was nominated for an Edgar Award by the Mystery Writers of America. She is the editor of *The Cambridge Companion to American Crime Fiction* (2010), as well as two volumes of reprinted novels by Anna Katharine Green and Metta Fuller Victor (Duke University Press).

Henry Sutton
University of East Anglia

Henry Sutton, SFHEA, is Professor of Creative Writing and Crime Fiction at the University of East Anglia. He is the author of fifteen novels, including two crime fiction series. His is also the author of the *Crafting Crime Fiction* (Manchester University Press, 2023), and the co-editor of *Domestic Noir: The New Face of 21st Century Crime Fiction* (Palgrave Macmillan, 2018).

Advisory Board

About the Series

Publishing groundbreaking research from scholars and practitioners of crime writing in its many dynamic and evolving forms, this series examines and re-examines crime narratives as a global genre which began on the premise of entertainment, but quickly evolved to probe pressing political and sociological concerns, along with the human condition.

Cambridge Elements ☰

Crime Narratives

Elements in the Series

Forensic Crime Fiction
Aliki Varvogli